# PRICE OF AD

# PRICE OF ADMISSION

## SAM EISENSTEIN

SUN & MOON PRESS
NEW AMERICAN FICTION SERIES: 25
Los Angeles

Sun & Moon Press
A Program of The Contemporary Arts Educational Project, Inc.
a nonprofit corporation
6026 Wilshire Boulevard, Los Angeles, California 90036

First published in paperback in 1993 by Sun & Moon Press
10  9  8  7  6  5  4  3  2  1
FIRST EDITION
© Sam Eisenstein, 1993
Biographical information © Sun & Moon Press, 1993
All rights reserved

This book was made possible, in part, through a grant from
the California Arts Council, the National Endowment for
the Arts, and through contributions to The Contemporary
Arts Educational Project, Inc., a nonprofit corporation

Cover: Roger Brown, untitled
reproduced by permission of the artist
and the Phyllis Kind Gallery, Chicago
Design: Katie Messborn
Topography: Rebecca Evans Associates

LIBRARY OF CONGRESS CATALOGING IN PUBLICATION DATA
Eisenstein, Sam
Price of Admission
p. cm — (New American Fiction Series: 25)
ISBN: 1-55713-121-X
I. Title. II. Series.
811'.54—dc19
CIP
Printed in the United States of America on acid-free paper.

*For my daughter, Chana*

*The deceased human being becomes the sole spectator of a marvelous panorama of hallucinatory visions; each seed of thought in his consciousness-content* karmically *revives; and he, like a wonder-struck child watching moving pictures cast upon a screen, looks on, unaware, unless previously an adept in* yoga, *of the non-reality of what he sees dawn and set.*

—Lama Kazi Dawa-Samdup as dictated to W. Y. Evans-Wentz

# PART I

## DEATH STALKS BRUNETTE IN GLOOM OF ALL-NIGHT MOVIE

The body of an attractive, well-dressed brunette, about 30-years-old, was found between two rows of seats in an all-night S. Broadway theatre at 4 a.m. today.

Both wrists were slashed. A stream of blood had trickled down the incline of the theatre's auditorium to form a pool 35 feet away.

The body was found by a patron, Claude R. Williams, 2108 S. Maple St., as he was leaving the theatre.

The house lights had just gone up after final screening of "The Track of the Cat," a gloomy psychological western film.

Manager Clarence Warner of the Moxie Theatre said the house lights had last been up at 3:30 p.m. yesterday.

Police said the woman apparently committed suicide by slashing her wrists with a razor blade and then slowly bled to death as the picture and its companion feature, "Crossed Swords," unreeled.

A black raincoat, a purse, and the razor blade were found alongside the body.

# ONE

D ark, with flashes of phosphorous, smoke entering the playing finger beam two bodies in height above the reclining seats.

Right handed finger manipulates a piece of gum still tacky and pliable, unseen felt remainder, chewed fast or slow, what kind of mouth, with or without teeth, before or after decision?

A seat filled with horsehair or settled fused air foam, polyethylene cover has cushioned how many sweaty buttocks in the dark anonymous. No history. Every night a different universe.

Lights go up at 7 in the morning until 8:30 am; then the sign turns on again: "Open—Always Three Big Hits."

On the floor above, a rooming house drains its residents from bottle to booth and into reclining chairs, luxurious, were luxurious, reminder of a time when the theatre showed first-run Ida Lupino and Rita Hayworth movies.

The screen is coated thousands of images deep. It should extend to take up all the room in the auditorium. Voices, soundtrack sprocket teeth in the projection room—how many thousands of miles of beautiful people it has passed like ammunition clips, shot at the screen, embedded.

Spring, winter, fall, summer, always the same temperature.

# TWO

——■——

A man enters the theatre. His name is Joe. He pays his silver. The woman in the booth issues him a ticket and tears it in half. He walks into the lobby. A sickle-shaped counter with candy and popcorn faces him. He must go around it in either of two directions, left to the water fountain and men's room, or right to telephone booth and women's lounge, then through the heavy black curtains into the auditorium. No sound from the auditorium can be heard next to the machines that keep popcorn popping, ice cream cold, lights bright. When the telephone operates there is a ring and a hum from the turning dial. If the man looks away from the counter his eye can feel the pulse of the fluorescent lights. In several places illuminated "exit" signs glow.

He has come west. The theatre is located as far west as it is possible to go on this continent. So he stops here, at the theatre, with three features going continuously all night and all day, except for one and a half hours in the morning, when everything piled up during the night is swept out into the street, into barrels or into the gutter and is flushed away into the sewers which go further west yet. But the man doesn't know about the sewer.

He might choose the sewer, if he knew it goes further west than the theatre.

He is very tired, in all the parts of his body where a man can be tired. But he does not sag. The tiredness is like a solid core in his body; it holds him up like an iron bar. The light flashing and changing direction from the projection room softens his tiredness until he molds himself to the reclining chair. It is always difficult for the Manager or Assistant Manager or ticket taker or candy counter woman—whoever's turn it is to stay until 7 a.m.—to detach him from the chair. He continues to look at the screen as though voices and bodies still come from it. But then he gets up and walks into the early morning before the traffic of business and banking companies starts and disappears into one of the openings in one of the buildings.

When he comes back his tiredness is much more rigid. He walks like a tin soldier. He could be placed like a rod between two chairs. Once the theatre had housed vaudeville. He might have volunteered to be the subject hypnotized, and prodded, sawed, bled between two chairs with a sequined-bottomed assistant sitting on his chest.

Joe enters the theatre. It is the time he always enters the theatre. But it is a different night. It is impossible for him to become more stiff. Tiredness has entered every finger of his hands. Silver tumbles out of his pocket to the floor. He walks into the theatre without a ticket. The ticket-woman walks out of her booth, recovers the change, puts it into a drawer. She does not give him a severed ticket. He walks to the left, into the auditorium. The Assistant Manager, sitting where he always sits, bows to the man slightly, as he does to regular customers. The candy counter girl and the Assistant Manager exchange a glance. But they do not speak. Nobody speaks in the lobby, no matter how many people are there. People pass through on their way to the auditorium where pictures are shown, or they buy confections, but the candy girl does not ask them what they want. She reaches into the refrigerated case or popcorn machine or soft drink mixer and hands out to the waiting hands what they need and then takes the silver, putting it into a drawer beneath the counter. Then people walk either to the left or to the right, either to the men's room and then into the auditorium, or to make a phone call and then into the auditorium, or into the women's room. The toilets have muffled flushers, so in the lobby it is impossible to know whether the toilets are flushed or not. The Assistant Manager goes into the men's room every hour he is on duty and checks on the toilets, the soap, the rotary towel. Then he relieves the candy counter girl and she goes every hour on the half hour to the women's room to check conditions there. But nobody checks the conditions in the auditorium where images flood the screen so many frames per minute, so many frames per hour, through the day and night, season after season. Only once a day, for an hour and a half, does anybody check the auditorium. Some of the people in the auditorium must be awakened and convinced it is time to go outside into the street that is beginning to be filled with pedestrians and motorists.

# THREE

J oe is very tired. He has never approached the candy counter for anything. The girl has never offered him anything from the counter. He always goes to the left, parts the heavy dusty curtain, disappears into the auditorium. He sits midway down and in the middle, directly under the heavy beam. He looks up into the light sometimes rather than at the screen. He seems to be able to read the image, cutting it transversely because of his long experience with images. He could have been in the projection room, film running in his hand, and seen as much with his fingers. He has never seen the man who runs the machines. The pictures are projected out of a little hole in the wall, but Joe has never been there to see how it works.

He has seen the large hexagonal metal cases in which the films are delivered. They stand on certain days outside on the sidewalk for a few moments until they are picked up. They are heavy cans and contain the week's films, thousands of feet and minutes, the only reason to be inside the auditorium devoted to shining images.

Joe is so tired he might have carried the film cases on his back. As though he had marched with the films from the manufacturer, where they were packaged and labeled, to all the theatres where they had ever been shown. Now that they had come to the three-feature film palace, he was very tired; he had chosen this place to be very tired in.

But Joe could not go on skirting the counter, rest rooms, telephone and water fountain, or the Assistant Manager who exchanged a look with the candy counter girl. He walks into the theatre without a severed ticket, parts the heavy curtains that are always dusty, and takes his place.

He has to decide, after having felt for the tacky gum left by him or someone else, just where to open himself so that the tiredness can flow out. He has spent many, many nights deciding just where the tiredness might flow out fastest. He decided finally on his toes, because they were closest to the floor and all of him could flow down to his toes with the least amount of labor. He opens each big toe, left foot and then right foot, and begins to feel tiredness flow out in two streams down the slope of the theatre auditorium. Over the steps, where there were steps, the two streams flowed apart and then together. Finally they come together beyond the seats in a space where there is nothing between front seats and the raised place on which the large silver screen stands. The blood collects there and stops.

By seven in the morning all the tiredness had passed from his body through his toes and down under the seats into the pool in front of the auditorium.

He is still sitting when the lights go up. The Assistant Manager and the candy counter girl enter the auditorium from either side and stop at his accustomed aisle. They walk from either end to the middle; each takes one of his arms and one of his legs. They carefully step over the seats with Joe in their hands. He is very light now that all the tiredness has passed through his toes, and they bring him down to the place in front where there are no seats.

Then they let him sit in the middle seat in the front of the theatre, a few feet from where all his blood is collected in a brown, rusty pool. His face, as they hold him over the pools reflects a dull red dim light. If the blood were frozen rather than only congealed, more of the details of his face might be revealed in it.

# FOUR

————

The blue face of the Assistant Manager was almost kindly. "Step over here," he intoned, glancing to the candy-counter girl to see if she were following and keeping tabs on the man.

Joe brought his face up from the mirror, annoyed at noting that he had another blackhead on his right nostril. "What is it?" He glanced in the mirror and saw both of them smiling at him, waiting for him to turn around.

"Say, what is this? What's she doing in the men's room?" Joe was belligerent. This wasn't a kinky theatre. She wasn't in drag. Neither was the other one. "Step over where?"

"Over to the Waiting Room," the Assistant Manager said, taking Joe's elbow.

Joe pulled away. The man's hand was uncomfortably hot on his elbow. The woman slipped out of the room.

"What time is it?"

The Assistant Manager glanced down at his wristwatch. "Mine has stopped," he said apologetically. "In the lobby there's a big one, based on the movement of the stars and sun. Accutron, I believe. The jewelry store down the street installed it recently. No more than one second off in every hundred years, or so they say." He laughed. "I don't expect to be around long enough to find out."

"I guess nobody will be, Joe said, more at ease. "I wouldn't want to stay in this lousy theatre long enough to find out when next week is."

"That's right," the Assistant Manager said. "Now, won't you come out this way?"

"Hey, I can find my way into the movie all by myself, I've been here before." Joe was all suspicion again. Something was fishy. He was being closed in on. The candy counter girl was back again. She was smiling at him. "How come you let dames in the men's room?"

The Assistant Manager and the girl exchanged another significant glance, shook their heads almost in unison. They looked so comical Joe broke into a laugh. He took another look at the black-head and turned briskly to the door.

The door swung to his hand, the automatic disinfectant dispenser wheezed, and Joe stepped out into the lobby. The lights were stronger than he had remembered. "Must have been real dim in the rest room," he thought. The fluorescent light in the center of the lobby pulsed, every pulse brighter than the one before. Joe began to grope with some panic to the familiar black, dusty drapes covering the entrance to the auditorium. If he could reach the place where the black curtains fell heavily apart in the center, he would be out of this clear, bright light. He would be home. He could sit in the center seat of the center row, the center of the beam from the projection booth, relax and enjoy the show.

What was the name of the first feature? The second? The third?

No way in. Joe's hand came onto clear, smooth surface. What? The glass counter top. The plastic side of the popcorn machine, hot, too hot for the hand. Stucco. The wall. The plastic of the telephone. Make a call. Joe groped for a quarter in his pocket. Smooth down his side. The pocket wasn't there. Sure it was there. He got the quarter out, dialed a number.

"Teresa. I'm at the show. Something's happened. You got to come get me. Something's wrong. I don't know what's wrong."

Joe listened. He heard a dial tone. He pressed the receiver down. Waited, dialed again. "Teresa?" Dial tone. He pressed the receiver again. The coin released and came down to his finger. The coin was old, smooth. But it had remained in the machine while he dialed. He put the quarter back into the slot, feeling for the right one, not the nickel or the dime, but the quarter slot. The coin fell in, stayed. He dialed. "Teresa?"

He must have the wrong number. Ask information. The blinding light. It was to keep queers in line. Nothing doing in *this* lobby. But his eyes must be going bad from sitting, watching.

The Assistant Manager's hand was at his elbow again. Joe shook it off. "Get your paws off me. I paid to get in here. I don't know you. I don't want your help. No, wait. Can you dial a number for me?"

"Of course," the Assistant Manager said. "What's the number?"

"How do I know you'll dial it for me?"

"Well, why shouldn't I? Teresa isn't in the theatre now, is she? Or could she be, and you're getting a no-answer signal? Perhaps Teresa is in the theatre right now? Would you like to go look for her?"

"How the hell can I look for her, I'm goddamned blind!" Joe yelled, afraid now that he'd said the word. Blind. Maybe blind for good.

"Come with me," the Manager said, "We'll go look for Teresa."

"No, I want to call her on the phone. I don't want her here. If I'd wanted her here I'd have brought her with me. She's in school. She's playing. She's at work. I call her when I need her. So I have to call her on the phone. That's why I have this quarter. Now will you take this quarter and put it in the phone and let me call Teresa?"

"Yes, give me the quarter." The Assistant Manager took the coin from Joe's jerky fingers. He put his hands over the fingers. Joe broke away and ran in the direction he hoped led to the doors to the outside. He held out his arms, expecting to encounter hard wood, metal, doorknob, or bar, to push, to thrust the door open into the sunlight, thousands of times less bright than this aching brilliance in the lobby. Smooth radiance on his hands as in his eyes. Another direction, smooth. Another. Smooth. Joe heard the Assistant Manager's quiet padding footsteps coming toward him after every pass. "I have your quarter, Joe."

"Then why don't you call Teresa for me? That's your job. You're supposed to help customers. Well, help me. I can't see. Something's gone wrong with my health. I was always healthy. I could see. Now I can't see anything. If you won't call Teresa, I want to get out of here. Show me the way to the door."

Joe listened for the steps of the Assistant Manager following him again. He heard nothing. Then a little steaming noise, and new popcorn began to pour out of the machine on the candy counter. Joe smelled fresh butter, salt. His mouth watered. "Say, let me have a box of popcorn instead. Teresa, she can wait."

"Of course." The Assistant Manager padded to the counter. "I'm giving you a smaller box, because the price is fifty cents, and you have only one coin, the one you gave me, isn't that right? So here you are, half a box of popcorn."

Joe groped for the box. He stuffed wads of popcorn into his mouth, gulped unpopped kernels between his lips, bit down on them, even on sensitive teeth. He felt no pain. He ate down the box and flung it away. He could not hear where it landed.

"Now you have no more money," the man said to Joe.

"No more money," thought Joe, "no more Teresa." He sat on his haunches and stared at the unfolding blue tapestry of the screen, an elongation of the Mercator map variety, as the teacher tapped on Baluchistan.

"Baluchistan, Afghanistan, Rajastan—which doesn't fit?"

"It isn't Rajastan—those don't go with the other ones," Joe yelled, sticking up his hand at the same time.

"Latvia, Lithuania, and—"

"Estonia," Joe yelled.

"Go home, Joe," the teacher said. "Go home, you have an infectious disease, foot in mouth," she hissed. "And your sister too, all the terribly intelligent little children of your race."

Ashamed. Race. Raced home. See Teresa. ("When?" inquired the Assistant Manager pleasantly. "None of your damned business.")

Run down the blue carpet, to fog rising from a field, whistle from thistle, thistle whistle and the dog, cog rail of Southern Pacific tracks over the rise of Truxtun and pennies on the track—Lincoln looked funny with his head pushed up like a coke bottle. Upon a penny, almost paper thin, trains thundering clack-clack. Once a face as Joe stooped to watch the wheels turn between the wheels, a bearded face. Joe threw a rock. Commotion. Red. Tumbling. He ran home, hid in Teresa's closet, in among the ammonia-smelling underclothes, powdery dresses, mothballed coats.

Summer. Simmer. The summing up, blue as eggs in the sky, reeds in the vacant lot.

"And Teresa? Do you still want to make the call? I can allow you one quarter, for one call," the Assistant Manager's voice smiled.

"Sure, I'd like to call. But she makes me sick. She's waiting for me to call. Sure, I'll call," Joe said. He was dizzy. Feeling sick. Too much wine. Blinded, but probably only a broken blood vessel. Shouldn't have looked so long, so closely at the blackhead on the side of his nose. Which side? Wouldn't that make a difference as to which eye would be most affected? He felt on his face for the blackhead. The nose was smooth. The Assistant Manager's palm was smooth. He became asphalt in summer, under the roaring asphalt fire of the road repair, the inferno of an asphalt layer. He lay on the floor of the lobby, no place to go. He felt the fire iron him until all was as smooth as wall, door, the palm of the Assistant Manager's hand, the well-worn quarter. Teresa was smooth too. The candy counter top was smoother than ice. He slid over its top onto the floor. He was smoother than beaten gold, than a jet contrail. He was elongated from the lobby to Teresa.

# FIVE

H e slipped out of the hand. Several hands were outstretched to catch him, but he eluded them. He would get to Teresa. Teresa, bound on the two arms of her name, he followed her whenever she moved from rooming house to dormitory, to another city. Always the same phone number, but another area code. No more money, not one quarter. "Damn the luck—how much does a quart cost now?" Used to end up with two quarters, one for popcorn, and the other for Teresa to come and get him in the morning on her way to work, her long old sedan moving slowly over and around the filled to overflowing trash bins and garbage pails. He could see her far away down the boulevard, picking her way with the big Packard sedan, blunt-nosed like a big watchdog. She would get out and check the trash for something usable while the car waited or moved ahead slowly until she made a little hop to catch up to it. The car never actually stopped for Joe. He caught it on the run, and Teresa took him to where he could stay for the day. Then in the evening they took him back to the theatre.

"Teresa, what do you do during the day?"

Teresa let the steering wheel hum its power steering and turned to him with her big Woolworth plastic sunglasses.

"Joe, baby, it's a long world, and there's 400 horses under this hood. I've got to let them go wherever they want to, and I don't know where that will be. I can't take you, so don't ask, don't ever ask. I pick you up, and I leave you there."

"Teresa, drop me off at a different theatre tonight."

"No."

"Teresa, I'm sick of the same goddamned movies. And the stiffs there spook me. They never say anything. I never say anything. Give me some more money for wine. I never have more than two quarters in my pocket. They're raising the price to get in."

"No."

"They are. They said so. There was a notice in the window this morning; they're raising the prices, effective November 1."

"It's May now. It's now the first of May. Spring is in the parking lot. The Packard's horses stomp and pant. I have to use Ethyl in May. I can't afford to give you more money. In the fall everything dies back and I can use Regular. If they raise the prices then, I'll give you more money. Find something in the back seat you can use to eat on."

Joe rummaged. A lampshade with a name and number on it, a pair of rubberized pants with a hole through the right pocket and another hole down near the knee, an electric train caboose with the initials T. J. scratched into the roof, the root of a calendula tied with wire painted white. "Nothing here this morning."

"Then you'll have to take what's in the brown bag and make it do."

Joe sighed. He took the bag, swung the door open as it passed the theatre, and hopped out. The pain in his right leg was worse, and stepping hard on the foot and toes made it worse every evening. The neon lights never changed. He didn't notice the name of the triple bill.

Teresa drove on slowly. Joe tried to step aside from the black exhaust, the fumes making his head as usual blow up with a headache that exhausted him and kept him in a stupor for whole minutes inside the theatre. That was why he never said anything to the girl who took the tickets, to the man who tore them, to the candy girl at the candy counter and the Assistant Manager who smiled. Teresa, Joe supposed, went to the theatre when he wasn't there, since she was able to discuss intelligently with him the plots of all the films. She knew the names of the actors, actresses, and directors of all the films. Joe sat beside Teresa on the freeway as they drove through the interchange to a suburb, where they stopped in front of a different house every morning for Teresa to explain the night's films. She could have written a book.

"Teresa, why don't you write a book? Then we could get in for nothing. You're wasting your talent."

"Here's the brown paper bag. And there's the theatre. Don't make us wait."

"O.K., Teresa. But if I need you, I'll call."

"You call, if you need us. But don't call if you don't."

Joe never called before the blindness episode. He never spoke to the Assistant Manager, which was a glorified name for all-around errand boy. He had no respect for such people. They were functionaries. He never needed them before. He had Teresa, who provided for things. But now he was blind, stretched over the counter, reaching in some blind way the distance between phone and restroom.

He had to crawl down and get into the auditorium.

People were trying to prevent him from getting inside to his place. Their smooth, lineless palms were feeling his face, poking around his pockets where the hole was, down by his knee cap where they had no right to probe.

He jumped over the roof of the caboose and down the other side to the railing. He flattened his body in the dark so that even a flashlight might have slid by in the murky night without revealing his whereabouts. He chuckled almost out loud at his cleverness. They wouldn't catch him. Now he could make a dash for it into the auditorium.

"There he is," Joe heard the Assistant say to the candy counter girl. "Don't let him get in. He hasn't any right to get in. He's been in there. Now he has to stay out here in the lights, until it's all set up. Hold him while I call for the others."

Joe heard all this while the tracks sped under him, while he waited for the slow-down to jump into the cinders. But the train continued to speed, diesels sounding like they were geared to cross the Tehachapis, maybe two or three engines together. If he jumped now, he would break every bone.

"You can't make it, Joe," the Assistant Manager said, his voice smiling, his meaning clear. He meant to keep Joe in the lobby until he would bring someone to hit him over the head. Joe remembered their carrying his head bobbing and bloodless out of the seat. They didn't care how hard he bumped against the unpadded seats. They never cared afterward. He was supposed to sit quietly while they did things about him behind the counter where nobody was allowed to go except authorized personnel. Joe couldn't see behind the counter even though he was high enough up on the glass, and could feel the heat of the lights underneath that kept the goods illuminated. But he couldn't reach through the glass, although he was hungry and had lost the brown paper bag somewhere along the way—maybe in the rest room—and he couldn't reach behind the counter into the case because it was closed in some ingenious way so that only the girl could press and slide, hook or unhook it, dispensing the goods, the candy.

The only chance he had, he thought, was to make himself thinner and thinner until he looked like glass wax on top and thus delude the eyes of the personnel. Then he would scrape his way into the theatre and be safe. There they couldn't go. Only when they got somebody outside in the bright lights did they have jurisdiction.

"It's not true, Joe. We can go in there too. Didn't we go in and get you?"

"Yeah, but I let you. I saw myself in the pool, and that's the permission. I know what the rules are. I didn't know before, but now I know what the rules are, and Teresa is coming for me in the Packard. She's probably outside right now, and the car doesn't wait. Because it's May and the Packard runs on Ethyl in May. That's why I just had one quarter, and now that's gone. You tricked me. I didn't need any popcorn. I had my brown paper bag, and now the bag and the popcorn and the quarter are gone. Because of inflation, and prices going up."

"That's only in the fall," the Assistant Manager said. "We like to give our clients ample time to make arrangements for the higher price. And we don't go up very much at a time. Not like other places. The price goes up gradually, so that people, our clients, can make the adjustment. Then they can sit and not worry about money. We like everybody to be comfortable. Are you comfortable now, Joe? Would you like to lie down? We have a lounge. I don't think you've ever been to the lounge. It's a beautiful lounge, where there are many people lounging, but they won't bother you."

"Keep your hands off my knee cap. I'm poor but I'm proud. I have connections. I don't need your crummy lounge. I paid to get into the theatre. Let me in the auditorium now, and I'll pay you again, since I guess it's another day now. Is it another day? Is it after 7:30?"

"Yes, it's after 7:30, and there's nobody in the theatre, or on the screen. The janitor is cleaning the theatre, scraping."

"Teresa can put it all up again. You should hire her. She knows all the ropes, all the pictures just like she was in them personally. I'll go get her. She's probably outside right now if it's around 7:00. Wait a minute."

The Assistant Manager's hands were at Joe's temples, but he brushed them aside. Joe's temples felt like quicksilver when the Assistant Manager's hands touched them, as though they could go right through into the back of Joe's throat. Joe swallowed, wanting to feel the heavy weight of a full bottle against the back of his throat, pressing down on his gums, while his throat worked to take the liquor down hardly even swallowing.

Joe's gums tingled when the nipple teased them. His nose was full, he had a cold. It was hard to suck. He cried without tears—his whole face got hot. Something put a hand on his hair. He cried harder. Steam helped. Headache. Nothing knew. He kept it. Light gave him headache, the glass was too hot, kernels of unpopped corn stuck to the back of his throat, the exact opposite of something warm and wet. No more crying, his face was not hot, no blood pumping into his head. That was in the theatre. Mirror and brown pool.

"Joe," the Assistant Manager reminded, "we have the authority. No use holding back. I offered to call Teresa. She won't answer, she knows the rules. She's been there. Come down off the counter."

# SIX

J oe clutched his heart half-theatrically, half in earnest. He was on a glass and rubbish littered street. His heart lifted. Was it Teresa? She turned bright lipsticked faces down on him. Her tailored suit with its knife-sharp lapels trained itself on his front. She crouched a little more easily to penetrate with the knives.

The spell passed. She was bored. Joe stared into the window of a men's shop, trying to decide whether Teresa was playing a trick on him. The lady's suit was on display, covering a manikin with a conspicuous bulge in the region of the cardiac. Joe was embarrassed, but so interested he couldn't look away. He didn't know what he would say to the woman when he turned from the manikin. Why the bulge in the region of the cardiac? It wasn't the cardiac anyway—that was when something was wrong—then they called it a cardiac case. It was the heart. What was so embarrassing about looking at an exposed heart? An advertising scheme, to sell suits. They had sold one to the lady.

The woman said: "If we're going to meet your little girl at the restaurant, we'd better hurry."

The woman was, then, an agent of the Assistant Manager.

Teresa wouldn't be at the restaurant, because he hadn't called her. How would she know? At every corner Joe hoped to find a telephone booth intact and not broken with glass splinters ready to penetrate his broken soles. The shoes were soft and tapered, almost blunt on the front edge, soft camel skin covering some kind of composition that allowed perspiration to enter and leave without trace. Joe was proud of his dry and odorless feet. Nothing was needed to preserve his blue-veined, wiry-strong feet, like good marbled beef, the kind you know is good.

Pain grew in the region of Joe's cardiac. The woman put on a soft felt hat, taking it from the crook of her arm, and walked away down the street of broken windows and long glinting pieces of glass. She walked through them without kicking but also without getting out of the way.

"Hey," Joe started. He followed, wincing from pain caused by the bulge in his cardiac and the glass slivers gathering and humping up at his toes. The pain was similar at both ends. His head was on fire too, and Joe wondered how there could be so much blood gathered at the base of his neck, the top of his spine, when so much of it was running out at his toes and gathering in a knot at his cardiac.

"Arrest," Joe yelled. The woman stopped without turning her head. Joe painfully caught up. Sunset was arriving high over broken gargoyles and copper rain spouts. Red clouds gathered. Joe was not unaware of the time—later than possible to get Teresa on the phone. He scanned the littered road, almost indistinguishable from the sidewalk. Only the Packard would make it over a street like this, and even with the Packard Teresa wouldn't be able to search over all the streets where he might be. The woman was about to start again and would get to the restaurant without him.

He could go with her, as she still seemed willing to be followed, granted his feet and cardiac arrest allowed for it. If he could live long enough to get to the restaurant, there was a kind of hope he could offer himself. But if he bled to death and the shoes were ruined, nothing much mattered. Teresa could search forever and never get to him. On the other hand, if the cardiac ceased, so would the blood. So he must keep that going, even if it meant doing all kinds of stupid tricks.

How he hated to keep a lady's attention by acting the buffoon. Joe sighed, tried to front the woman on his right side, so the bulge wouldn't be so visible, and sidled some steps with her. He had to skip away and hide behind almost every facade, and that took every bit of energy. Never before had he realized the ounces and grams of life. He made a resolution never again to mention, even mentally, the words, as other words drained from his pores and followed the first, unobserved ones, into the gutters, down the seats, aisle after aisle, to the pool at the front of the theatre.

Her precise tweed was straight-lining the sidewalk again as Joe feinted and dodged, smiling with white gums and light head. Naturally, as she didn't turn back, she couldn't see Joe's smile, nor even remark his wasteful motions. Sooner or later, if life endured, they would arrive, at approximately the same time, at the restaurant. A vast place, on one floor, with one waiter every four tables. Joe sat. The woman smiled, opened her shiny bag, and knew exactly where her lipstick was. She opened and applied it, while Joe tried to focus on the menu.

"Teresa ought to be here very soon," he said, but everything was a dim network of blood in his eyes. Joe tried to see if the blood was really spurting from his eyes onto the starched tablecloth, or whether the veins were magnifying themselves on the white screen for his benefit and were in reality very very small. He turned to ask the lady. She was putting on the lipstick, red, thick, shiny. It pooled on her mouth. She stuck out her tongue—much pinker and easily defined as a tongue, but then the whole mouth became a pool of red, an eye.

He shook himself, regretted it, as he was terribly porous. Shaking a sponge is not a good idea. If Teresa came they would make a fresh start. They would talk it over. He would clean out the Packard, even the glove compartment and the seat well. There were hidden places in the Packard that he would search out. It was a good sound car.

There was a man in the corner by one of the colonnades. He winked and grinned with tiny milk-teeth, like scissors. The lady got up and went behind the column, pretending to adjust a stocking. She showed her mouth to the man, spread her lips, pressed them down and up on one another, even displaying her tongue, the inner gums and tonsils, all the soft erectile tissue that lets go of each other only with effort, effort a dying man cannot afford to expend on his mouth to make the jaws separate. Still, she would not raise the stocking on her cold mutton leg without going behind the column.

The waiter came with poised pencil. The bulge was greater than before.

"I need, at least, some coffee."

"Some coffee, sir? You're not having dinner with your companion?"

"Yes, of course I am. But some coffee first, please."

"Yes, sir, and some popcorn, may I suggest popcorn?"

The waiter's face twisted in a sardonic smile. Only then did he reveal his gums, his hands free of the starched cuffs shooting toward Joe. No, toward Joe's menu, to take it away. Joe clutched his menu. They struggled for the menu.

"I will bring it back, sir; never fear, I will bring it back. Please give me the menu. Our specials and our prices change from hour to hour, so if you don't order now, I will bring you another version of the menu.

"I'll see if the candy counter girl has any, and if she can give some up," the waiter said. "Would you like to come with me?"

Joe pretended to get up, so the waiter would turn his back, but the floor was slippery—he didn't dare look down to see what made it slippery, and he could get no purchase. He did get the waiter to turn his back, and so he slipped to the floor under the table, hoping that when the right pair of legs approached he would be able to stop them and identify himself. He may have gone to sleep.

# SEVEN

Wrathful. They pursued him, the little brown children. "Jesus!" They shrieked. Joe wondered if he were Jesus. "Jesus."

The church lurched toward Joe on tall legs, like water-skimmers, two eyes skewed in his face. Bells breathed soft rapping noises at him. Joe ran toward the church, the church ran toward Joe. They ran into each other.

Joe as church stood and waited for the tormentors. The children ran up and down his entrance. Joe put out a step. "Ow!" a tough little boy cried.

"What happened?"

"It bit me."

"We'll have it in for excommunication. Priest-killer!"

Everything was fine. As church Joe could eat popcorn all day long, on Sunday wafers. They sent current through his veins, the electric bells rang on important days, when someone died or was born. Teresa and the Packard described complicated circles in the square. The movie house? Unbuilt. Time passed. Joe settled in, worried about the sub-basement not sunk deep enough into the mud. He moved his toes. He could move his toes.

He should not be able to move his toes. He tried to communicate with the people who ran the church on his behalf. They were not listening. They were old and crying to heaven for protection from marauders. The brown boys grew up. They took to throwing grenades at Joe's midsection. He marveled how they never forgot.

Didn't they have jobs and illnesses, mistresses, movies to see? Joe decided it was the fault of television. "Never had television when I was a kid," he thought. "Teresa," he boomed on his bells. But it was one of those times she wasn't there. The Packard had to be fed, and the church was nowhere near a gas station. Joe suspected that Teresa had an arrangement with the gas station attendant, who had been there pump in hand for as long as the station.

Joe sent a church member to the gas station. He came back and got into a confessional.

"What happened there?" Joe asked.

"I went over to the gas station, and there was this lady looked like a witch. I crossed myself and the man splashed gasoline on me and tried to light it. I told him I was an authorized messenger."

"What happened then?"

"The lady said, 'Tell Joe all this is useless. I can't come anymore.'"

"Did you ask her why?" Joe squeezed the room in on the parishioner until he gasped. He reminded Joe of one of the former children.

"Oh stop. I asked her why. She said that you'd have to come out, that it was wrong, you're wasting time."

"Who else was there?"

"There was a man, kind of bald, smiling all the time, and a tall girl who stood behind him."

The Assistant Manager and the candy counter girl! So they were in it together. With Teresa! With the Packard! Simple betrayal, no question about it. They were plotting.

Joe crushed the man. Then he ate him. He took the usable portions into his mortar and the liquid into his veins.

"I can't do that many more times," he thought. "They'll miss someone coming out of confessional, they'll see that the outside has a glow after someone comes in here. Someone will suspect. Teresa already knows. O Teresa, seductress, betrayer. You I thought I could trust. You I thought would understand why I came to this."

Joe withdrew from the room and stationed his eyes in the belfry, waiting for a sign.

They were in the square many hundreds of feet below, lined up: brown men, the Packard, Teresa, all of them. They had dynamite. The place was cordoned off. Police guarded all four corners. A crowd strained toward the building. Priests swung censers filled with sweet smoke. Popcorn vendors scored, yellow-white boles billowing from their fingers, transferred to open hands and mouths. The square looked like a sheep's back.

"Out, evil spirit, out!" the priests intoned.

"Never!" cried Joe. "I paid my dues. This place is in great shape. What do you want from me?" No one listened.

Joe saw one shape detach itself from the rest, break through the lines and run toward the entrance of the church. It was far, and Joe's eyes were none too good at midday when there were no shadows. The figure ran, a two-dimensional dot, across the pavement. Joe saw smoke, heard a shot, the figure stumbled and fell, got up again, crawled toward an entrance.

Joe sympathized, tried to put out a wall to protect the figure, but he was too late. All that he was able to do was let drop some bricks on the already hurt man who shielded himself, made a fist at the building, and crawled the remaining steps into the building. Joe slammed his front door behind the man, while police pounded on the door, shot bullets into the lock to make it loosen, and then pulled back in a group to confer. Joe dropped a grillwork on the group. There was a shout as it came down, but the police didn't have a chance.

Joe felt the man run through his body, pulling himself up step by step with the leg that still worked, bleeding onto every surface he passed, pulling himself up higher and higher. Finally Joe was able to see him: the Assistant Manager.

They were face to face in the belfry. Joe was in the bells. He began to toll. He could see the words form on the wounded man's mouth. He wouldn't listen. There was no law that said he had to listen. The man went down on his knees and Joe saw that one knee was blasted to mush. He knelt on it anyway, and Joe understood that he must listen.

"All right, what is it? I don't have much time."

"It's true," the man said, his face still contorted from pain and the deafening sound of bells. "I can't hear myself speak yet, my ears are ringing."

"Well, I didn't ask you up here. You gathered all those people, didn't you?"

"Yes," the Assistant Manager replied, bald head shiny with exertion, sweat, blood, where he had wiped a hand fresh from his knee. "But for your good. This is not allowed. Escape is impossible. Sooner or later you have to come back. You have to go back to the starting place. This is wrong."

"Wrong or not, it's my way. How did you corrupt Teresa?"

The Assistant Manager looked interested. "That her name? She wouldn't tell us. I thought that was a taxi."

"No, you idiot," said Joe, "that's the Packard. Don't you remember she used to bring me to the theatre in it?"

"I never worked the box office," the man apologized. "I never noticed. If I had seen her, I would have remembered her. Fantastic woman."

Joe realized the depth of collusion. He moved the bell over the kneeling man and tolled him out. "One, two, three."

"Stop!" the man cried.

Joe continued grimly.

"I can make them all go away," he cried.

"But you won't. We'll all go together, in a mass. They'll excavate here and find a monument."

The Assistant Manager grew hair. His pants went away. He was wearing a dress. Teresa knelt in his place.

"About time you showed yourself. Explain all of this!" Joe said, sternly pointing at the square where there was a World War I cannon set up. It was sending absurd little puffs of smoke and rusty balls at the stained glass window. This time there was a direct hit; the crowd yelled, "Ole!" Joe flew razor sharp shards of glass into the crowd. It split like a melon and sent bright red seeds into the air. The eye of the crowd blinked. Hardly anybody has the chance to see a church crucified.

"You have no right to assume to yourself the role of judge," Teresa said.

"If I don't nobody does."

"Nobody you know, that is," Teresa replied. "But you don't know everybody, do you? In fact, you know hardly anybody. You've seen every movie ever made but that doesn't qualify you. You've done some of the right things, but now you're doing the wrong thing, and I can prove it."

"Go ahead and prove it."

"Do you remember draining in the theatre? Do you remember everything that happened there?"

Joe was trapped in the bells. He wanted to be out with Teresa. When she was trying to convince him of something she sometimes unbent, she would take off her clothes. Then Joe could see her navel and everything below the navel. "My god," Joe thought, "I sure wish I could do that now!"

"Joe, listen. This is very bad."

"What about the gas station? What did you do with the Assistant Manager?"

"That'll be all right. Just come out and let me talk to you. There isn't much time," she said, echoing the man before her.

"You're in it together. With the glass and mirrors, with those damned people who robbed me in the theatre. I wanted to go straight in and stay there and they threw me out."

"Nobody threw you out. I understand you had to come in here, but it's gone too far. Let's get out while there's still time."

"No, now you're really in for it. The Packard can't help you. If you don't take off your clothes I'll send a ton of bricks down on it and you'll never move again. One, two, three . . ." Joe counted with relish. Never had he had Teresa where she had to obey his commands.

"Here, here's my navel," she cried.

"No, all of it. All of it."

She ripped off her black dress. She took off the dress beneath it. Then another dress. She continued to disrobe while Joe counted. A shiver ran through the building. Some of the glass glowed and ran together in a fused mass. Some of the people were caught in the crazy colors of glass that had been stained windows. The new glass had lumps and texture, very artistic. Already there were dealers in the crowd down below, distinguishable by their clown costumes. They were bidding frantically for squares of substance. Relatives and survivors played them off against each other. Officers struggled to keep them from the glowing glass.

What if all the evidence were sold and carted off? Where would the authorities get proof that the glass had been people?

Joe looked back to Teresa. "Thirty, thirty-one, thirty-two . . . forty eight, forty nine." Teresa stood naked before him. Now it was Joe's turn to blink, close his eyes against the glare, the terrible light that pierced his metal to its center.

He shattered.

# EIGHT

I t was night. Light fell fitfully over the bodies, glowed in a rib-cage here, an empty eyesocket there. Teresa held Joe's hand. They stepped between flowing rivers of hair and fingers still clutching bits of dollar bills and coins.

Teresa was speaking earnestly and softly. "Rivers of turmoil. The universe will not blame you. It was all due, but now? Still, they could have gone on for a long time, a longer time. Do you remember the moment of the passing of light from your sockets?"

"Yes, " Joe answered, shortly. Did she think he was an idiot?

"You had time to think while the blood drained from your toes? Why did you do it?"

"I don't know. I did it to annoy you, I suppose. Black smoke, fumes. The screen was so thick there wasn't room in the theatre, and you wouldn't take me anywhere else," Joe said.

"It all comes down to this field."

That was indisputable, Joe thought. A field. Policemen gone or consumed, down into the dark. He looked up at his refuge. Blank and black. No moon yet. He felt a twinge of regret at allowing himself to be moved. He thought of the dark rooms, each with boards and bricks. He turned around. Teresa caught his elbow.

"You wanted me naked. Here I am."

Sure enough, she was still naked. Joe hadn't noticed, he was so busy looking at people sprawled in every conceivable position, in glass and out, still trying to attach themselves to each other to keep from being pulled into the moving river of colors. Now and then a hand with or without dollar bills clutched at Joe's ankle without strength. Joe looked everywhere for the brown boys who hated him; he couldn't be happy thinking they were putrefying in there without being sure.

"Let's lie down here," Teresa said.

"Here?"

"Why not?"

"It's too public. In the back of the Packard you never would. You wouldn't come into the theatre. Where you live you wouldn't even take me."

"Look at the people all around, do they look ashamed?"

Joe looked. They were pulsing like one great body, lights under and around their legs and thighs. The belly buttons, every one with a light in it, pushed aside by other bodies and the whole of them swamped by the river of fluorescent light.

"Let's go some place private," Joe said.

Teresa pulled him down on her. He felt something soft, something hard. Was it him? Which was him, the soft or the hard? "I'm a man, aren't I?"

"You are what?" Teresa said savagely.

She was taller than the steeple, her eyes deep and empty as telescopes. Far back, they glittered like hell pits.

"Come back, "Joe commanded, "or I'll leave again."

"Oh, watch the couples embrace," she called.

They were piled ten deep, concentrated, alive, every one of them smiling, smiling everywhere.

"Come on in, Joe, the water's fine, "several laughed, at Teresa's motion. "Teresa's really all right, she knows the score. Come on."

Joe rubbed his eyes. His fingers were glowing. The hell lights were on him too. He realized that if he joined the heap it would be to admit guilt. He would go the way of all those in the heaps streaming down to be consumed by the rivers.

"Not this time. I can hold my own. Ha. Ha." He laughed at Teresa, shrunk to her normal size, "Get the car. You get the car now. I'll do it all in my own time. You get the car, let it ride, and we'll get into the back seat."

"Joe, Joe," Teresa murmured, tears seeping out of her eyes, falling on the hot ground with a gentle hiss. "You've got to go through with it. Let yourself go. It's started, you've got to let it happen. Then we can be together again when it's all done."

"No ! " Joe shouted.

# NINE

"Teresa, come out," Joe called from moat-side of the turret. "Let down your hair." Sighed. Not giggled. Immature. Giggling denotes insecurity, incapacity. Laws of cause and effect. What's my trousers doing: Hard-on no, now, no coat to hide. "Teresa, what's keeping you?"

Light in the turret off. Flow of a body down stairs darker dark at each of the iron-barred windows. She stopped at the foot of the stairs, looked up at the sky. Patently, thought Joe, she knows I'm here. Patently.

She turned to him, caught one hand to her gossamer guersey, held out her other to be helped over the moat.

Patently, a fraud. What the hell.

"Teresa, here you are."

"Yes, I've come."

Not very far. Why did he have to wait so long every time?

"My father again, and my sister."

"What about them?"

Teresa held the scarf above the bridge of her nose, her eyes rolled at Joe. She weighed less than one side of Joe. Which side? Joe wondered, lateral or vertical?

"What about them?" He repeated, knowing that it would be something about the silver mine petering out again, or Indian raids.

"The mines and the Indian raids," Teresa said. "Father came home last night with horrible gashes across his insteps. My sister came down from the other tower for the first time since he's been away this time. He glared at her and swiped her across the face with his riding crop. She howled like a wolf."

"Fantastic," said Joe. "Let's go get something to eat."

"It'll have to be in La Cañada. They know something is happening. I can't vouch for your safety if they find out."

Joe held the door for her. Till eleven. He had the car. Hope no cop stopped them. No license. How long she'd want to stay in the restaurant, can we get to the Wash in time? Will she? Not sure I want. All those bones. Flesh. Hair like just out of waterfall. Grease? No, clean-smelling dry. Like a nest before the birds live in it. Made-up history. Never go back. Desert in Mexico. Girl rode away. Anchors aweigh. Into the car.

"Joe, Joe. Stop here. Tell me you love me. Tell me. Say it. Say you love me."

The signal going green, yellow, red. Green, yellow, red. Times four. "Yes, I care for you. Yes."

"Love. Say love."

"I can't. I can't be without you, but."

On the Bluff, rain and thunder, lightning and hail, dust storms and grit, sand and water, wind and everything.

Joe held her in his arms like a sacrifice. Teresa's little hands around his neck, hurting. On the cliff face.

"Jump!" she whispered.

"Teresa, sometimes you scare me!" It wasn't true. She never scared him. No more than an expensive vase suddenly balanced on his head.

She asked to be set down

"Extinguish the effects," she said. "I don't care about them any more."

Joe stopped the dust, rain, etc.

"I can't say more than I feel is honest," Joe said.

"Then you will not live," Teresa said, "you will not survive, and I will be a prisoner in the castle beyond the moat in my turret until my father comes back from Mexico with the husband he has chosen for me, and that will be the end of it, and the end of me."

He wanted to say, "And the end for me too," but couldn't. The car had to be returned before Alan's mother got home from work. A promise was a promise. Teresa, Teresa. "Teresa, Teresa."

"Say it," she whispered.

"I can't," he cried.

# TEN

"Keep your fingers out of my eyes, Teresa," Joe cried. "Get them out. Vengeful bitch."

She squeezed the matter out and the sky went restful for Joe.

"This is to give you a sampling of what happens when you don't obey the laws," she said. "I'm not doing this from malice. Someone has to take you in hand."

The Assistant Manager and the candy counter girl came over. The gas station attendant was there too, and the waiter. They stood in a ring around Joe. Joe felt each of their faces.

"Here is your mirror," said the Assistant Manager.

"Here's your clarinet and flute," said the candy counter girl.

"Here's a vase of flowers," said Teresa.

"Here's a little something to keep your appetite down," said the attendant.

"And a change of clothes," said the waiter.

"Shall we put him in the earth with the rest?" the candy counter girl asked.

"No, he'll go vampire, if I know him," Teresa said.

Joe's eyes were spread like paste along the inside lobe of the sky.

"God, I've got a headache," he said, feeling for Teresa's shape. The mass of them moved, he got hold of the Assistant Manager instead. He felt for his navel and the furry hair descending to his genitals. Joe reached down and held on—a way of escape, down. Nothing. Nowhere.

"Illusion, Joe, illusion. The whole thing is illusion."

"Teresa didn't trap me, did she? I didn't go along with it, did I? That's good for something "

"Good for what?" the Assistant Manager said. "How do you think you occupied the church, a body with balls. Think about it, and come away with us."

Joe's mind jumped in its cage like a maggot on a stove. One by one he heard a scream and felt a death. Each brain-maggot had a story and an image inside. Poverty-stricken brain, it still had pictures. He tried to see each one as it popped, screamed, turned black and gave over its tiny load of life. Billions disappeared before he had a chance to stop even one for examination. Why wasn't a man prepared for such things now that everybody was picking on him? He couldn't see the outside so he couldn't go anywhere. He had to rely on Teresa after all.

"Give me back my pictures."

The candy counter girl dropped a pail of ice on Joe's head. Now he could not even see the pictures as they died away, the maggots froze dead. They were emptying him of alternatives.

"How did I sin?" he cried.

"Well, one thing, you committed suicide," the gas station man said reasonably. "We sell gas for Packards and the like, but every other day now some young guy comes in dressed up in yellow or orange and buys half a gallon of Ethyl, with lead in it . . . 'You can't get the lead out,' I always say to these creeps. They don't say anything, just take the gas, pay the deposit on the can, which I make three times as high because I know I won't get it back, and they leave. Then I read about it in the paper next day. Unless I go along with the creep to watch. I'm watching now. I didn't see you do it but Assistant Manager here, he gets to me so quick, I'm almost in on it anyway. I'm almost always everywhere. Now I'm here, and I want to help you, Joe. You're not the first to want to turn back."

"No, I didn't know," said Joe. "I didn't know." He kneeled, sobbing. Everybody put hands on his shoulders. He wept harder. Suddenly, he grabbed hands and twitched them over his shoulders. He felt bodies rise and hit his head and go over to the smooth surface. He felt for two heads and smashed them together. Then two more, and smashed them. Oh he wanted to smash and to smash.

# ELEVEN

"So why didn't you stop me? You knew it already?" Joe snarled. "I'll tell you why. You didn't want to have the theatre cleared—it would have cost you money, isn't that it? And you never scraped the screen regardless of decency and regulations. In a little town a little girl is executing her doll for the benefit of pedestrians and highwaymen? I saw it from a hotel across the street from the post office. All night long people stuffed letters into slots—local, special delivery, air mail, foreign. Why didn't they wait until next morning? What were they afraid of? That they were going to disappear? Is that what they were afraid of? If I had stopped looking, the post office would have disappeared, into the clouds. I had to stay awake to help those people get their messages off before morning, so they wouldn't reread them. Maybe then they wouldn't have sent them after all. They would have thought twice. And on the other end? All those people not reading the night-screams of their friends, their lovers, their creditors, their enemies. I've done a few right things in my life, damn it. I don't deserve to be chained to a corpse. I did what I could for pigeons. I visited the palace of justice, I blew smoke into the mail slot, I did these things. Isn't it enough?"

"No."

"Here's your hobby horse back, Teresa. Don't go out today. Don't go near the street. The big horsies go there. Don't go near them, not this time. Wait until you're three feet tall, one meter.

Only one meter. No more. Gone. She's gone. Could I prevent it? I couldn't. Don't ask me."

"No."

"I did not desire her. That is a lie. There was no desire. I said, 'Run along.' I touched her along the shoulder blade. Nowhere else."

# TWELVE

"All right," the Assistant Manager said at last. "Now the innocent will commence to suffer. Hostages!"

They were at the theatre, everybody in the regular place, except that Teresa was parked at the curb in the Packard. The metal of the car went red, blue, green and black, according to the lights of the neon on the marquee. Teresa studied her fingernails.

# THIRTEEN

"All right," the Assistant Manager said from his director's chair, "take it again. Joe, you're sitting on the bed with Teresa, explaining to her why you've stepped out on her. She's crying, not hard, just tears rolling down her cheeks. Go from there. Camera. Lights. Action."

Old men and derelicts sat in their seats like stuffed dummies or manikins in cheap stores, eyes open but seeing nothing. Joe's eyes worked again. He blinked them to make sure, felt the balls and winced as his gritty fingers made little stars where they touched. He ran his tongue over his lips—rouge and makeup. Teresa sat completely at her ease.

"I've got to. . . ." he started.

"I'll never be able to trust you. . . ." she said.

"They inspire. . . ."

"Dirty little. . . ."

"They don't. . . ."

"I feel. . . ."

"Cut," the Assistant Manager said. "There's no honesty in either of you. Candy," he called to the back of the theatre. "Come out here. You do it with her. Joe, step aside. Go over to the lobby "

Joe grinned. Now he knew the game. "Huh uh," he said. "No dice." He walked over to the Assistant Manager and squatted on his haunches. "I stay with you."

"All right, stay with me. Jesus, Joe, if you only realized we're trying to help you. For God's sake."

"Sure you are."

Candy said, "I do love you."

Teresa said, "But I don't haunt your imagination when we're not together."

Candy: "But you are my wife, the companion of my life. I've got to project things onto the other girls, the long-haired honey-colored girls."

Teresa: I'll never trust you. I can't let myself go with you, and then you complain I'm cold. I start to get warm and then I remember you've been in bed, probably even this bed, with those. . . ."

Candy: "They inspire me—even to disgust—something is released, then I can live, even when I hate myself. I project myself onto them—it's nothing personal. I don't even like them. I like you."

Teresa: "They're dirty and cheap. They laugh at you behind your back. You're just practice for them. They don't take you seriously, and you believe you're some sort of hero."

Candy: "They don't do that. I don't know what they want, but it's not that."

Teresa: "I feel so cheapened by you and your sneaky adventures. You talk about projections and soul and your 'mission' in life, but all you do is try to get in bed with the easiest and sickest girls. You cater to rotten fruit."

Joe slumped to the floor. He considered opening his toes again. But as he looked down he saw that they gaped like the fronts of worn-out shoes. The cuts were white like bleached flour. There was no blood to run. He felt his arms—tendons and muscles hanging from bone. He reached to the Assistant's neck with one hand. He took hold with both hands and squeezed while the man made whimpering noises.

"Joe, Joe, stop it, we've got the next scene to run. It isn't my life."

Joe squeezed while he looked up at the stage where Candy and Teresa were frozen. Candy had hands around Teresa's neck. Every time Joe squeezed harder, Candy did the same. Teresa was dying. Even Joe could see that. Abruptly, he released the Assistant's neck. Joe pinched his nose to clear his head. "What are you making me do?" he cried.

The projectionist-cameraman stuck his head out of the slot in back of the theatre. "Shall I keep that?" he called.

"Sure," said the Assistant. "Pretty good."

Joe felt faint. If he had had any blood he would have been blushing. But he couldn't blush. "I'm a fool. I choke you and I am choked. I hit her and I'm hit. What's the use?"

Teresa shaded her eyes against the bright lights. "So why do you do it? Why can't you think first before you cause trouble?" "I'm not causing any trouble. There wasn't any use. Day after day the same thing. What else is there besides wine and the movies? Nothing changes. Everything was decided before I was born. I never had a chance."

Candy came down. "Shall I give him an ice cream?"

# FOURTEEN

"Strychnine for you, but don't swallow it until you get home."

"Can I give it to my mother?"

"Sure, you can give it to anybody you want to, but remember, it's permanent."

Another little boy came up to the candy counter. "What else do you have beside poison and candy?"

"We have ice cream. "

"What flavors?"

"Every flavor. You make them up in your mind."

"Does it go with the movie?"

"There aren't any movies today."

"There aren't? How come we paid to get in here if there aren't any movies?"

"You're going to live here now."

"That's OK, I don't like living at home. What do I have to do, living here?"

"Clean everything. All the time. Everything has to be transparent and clean, so that the people can look in and admire the place."

"It doesn't look so clean to me."

"That's to you. Didn't you already eat the candy?"

"Sure. "

"Then you know what goes on here. You'll never leave again. Some days we show movies and you'll think you're on the street, but you won't be. In fact, you won't remember what I'm telling you right now. Nobody does, not all the people who are walking outside right now. They're really in here with you." "There isn't that much room in here." "There's all the room in the world." "Out of sight." "Right."

# FIFTEEN

"We're showing porno flicks today," the cameraman said in great excitement.

"No kidding!" Joe said. "Naked ladies."

"Yeah, naked ladies. We got them from the Museum of Modern Art. Try sleeping with one of those three-faced women. What they've got down below after we've scraped off the paint you wouldn't believe."

"Will I see it?"

"You'll see it. We get all the rejects. The management had the chance to go to bed with the most beautiful women in the world but they decided to buy pictures of them instead. More lasting power." He laughed. "Well, they're all here. They'll never leave again."

Joe took his arm. "Tell me the truth, man, does everybody live here?"

"No, not exactly here. Around here. Well, I've got to go scrape. I'm always scraping, scraping. I don't know what I ever did to deserve this."

"Where did you come from?"

"Which time, Joe? Which time?"

# SIXTEEN

"A long trip, Joe," the attendant said, "I've got the gas ready for you. You don't even need coupons."

Joe scratched his head. "How do I know you know what you're doing? How much gas is it?"

"What kind of car you got?"

"An old Packard. I can't afford anything newer on my salary. Doesn't get many miles to the gallon."

The man winked at him. "Doesn't matter how far you go, you got sealed orders, don't you? Intact, with the seal on? Sign here."

Joe took the official paper covered with seals and indentations and a little crossed blue ribbon. The writing looked like snakes. Joe's bad eyes saw it move. He put the papers on a ledge. The wind riffled them. He hoped they would fly off the ledge into the sea. The wind pushed the hair into his eyes, but the papers sat there like lead.

"How do I know I can get back?"

"You don't, nobody does. It's the judgment."

The attendant stood in the entrance of the cave with a stave. Every time Joe approached to hear him better he jabbed with the stick and giggled. He held out the can of gas. "Not in here, Joe. Not this way."

Joe took the can of gas from the ground. Suddenly he flung the can at the man, hitting him in the stomach. The attendant got up and sloshed gas over himself, took a match and lit himself. He went up like a wooden match, light from him illuminating about a dozen feet into the cave. Joe saw with double vision the burning man and the cave wall, covered over with remarkable colored images of all the people he had ever known. He saw his future in lines like the veins on the inside of his eye, all going up in fire and smoke. He tried to smother the fire with sand, but the man smiled and burned, still guardian, still holding his stick.

The fire burnt down. The stave remained. There was no set of orders on the ledge. It was gone if not burned. Joe cried. "My house is gone. My past is burned. Why do I make mistakes like that? I'm sorry, I never knew you well, I never wanted to, I didn't trust you. Now it's too late."

"Cut. Cut," The Assistant Manager said. "Douse Saint Anthony. We'll have to print it, we're running out of film. Do you hear that, Joe? We're running out of film. We've got to make every take count. It's too late to redo most of the scenes. The screen's covered with them."

Joe, feverishly: "Why not scrape them off, like I said before? I know how to do it, at least I know Teresa can do it."

"She's asleep. She's tired. You wear her out. She can't always take care of your dirt for you, Joe. Let her alone. Let her sleep. She's tired."

Sure enough , Teresa was lying in the seat Joe always used to sit in, and she was asleep.

# SEVENTEEN

"Do you remember," Teresa asked, "when you fell into that store where the man had a free lunch?"

"No," Joe answered. "I don't remember that."

"I didn't think you would. You were greedy for the free lunch and chewed on some things, and then you noticed that the proprietor had snails crawling up and down his vest. He opened the drawer of his cash register and we saw snakes crawling around in there."

"The store was very dark?"

"Yes, almost total darkness. But we could see the snakes and the snails. You said, 'My god, I'm eating snails then?' And I laughed. The man and his wife laughed, and the woman ran across the dusty road to the ocean where she pulled out some octopus and carried it back. The man put it on his vest too, where it was like a star to the snails' glistening rays. You couldn't swallow what you had in your mouth. You wanted me to put it in my purse so you wouldn't embarrass anybody."

"I never did that."

"Oh yes you did. You wanted to put whatever you couldn't carry into my purse. I was gay about it. I held the purse open, but when you went to spit the mess into it, it fell on the floor beside the trough. The woman had just come back into the room. She was standing at the door. She saw what you did and her smile faded like the sun. The man just stood there, stoic." "That must have happened to him a lot, serving up snails to guests."

"We weren't guests, we had just broken in and he was being nice. You spit it all out on the floor. You said something inane: 'Well, I've got to get back to the railroad track and wait for the train.' The man just stood there nodding his head and smiling. His wife didn't say anything. She just waited in the door. You brushed past her, grinning and bobbing, working your mouth to get the remains of the snails out of your teeth. All I could do was go with you and mumble apologies. We had no right to be there if we weren't going to he thankful for the snails and the octopus. Do you remember?"

"No. Don't make up my past. You always try to convince me of how I was wrong. You can't do that to me."

Joe turned away from her and went to sit in another part of the theatre. Teresa, he saw, had not moved. In fact, she had been asleep all the time. Joe's scalp crawled.

# EIGHTEEN

—————

J oe stands on the bank of a little stream. Hollywood in the good
old days, before talkies. Joe was safe in whatever he said;
nobody was around to record it. But as the thought came to him,
he realized that everything is recorded, on camera. He was long in
the future and still in the past. He was stretched on a rack. The
events of the in between punctured him like computer cards, but
he couldn't decode them. He knew the outcome, but he couldn't
come out there until he had lived the intervening years. He was des-
perately hungry for Teresa, but was she born? Where was she born?
In Sioux City, Iowa. How could he get to Sioux City without
money, with clay feet, steeped in this little stream? What good
would it do if he went to the pregnant woman, Teresa's mother,
and said: "I'm Joe. Let me in." Let me in—what? He would have
to wait while she went through her childhood, her infancy, her ges-
tation, her insemination. He would go to Teresa's father, smoke
cigars with him, maybe he would give Joe a job, and wait with cigar
in hand on events.

A pump is throbbing at the dam-end of the little stream. Making electricity. enough power for the time.

A little house—Teresa in there. A little dog barks at the window,
chintz curtain flapping lazily in the breeze.

The stream is a snarling torrent. The little motor works hard,
then misses a beat. Goes on. Suddenly it stops, the level of water
rises, laps the bottom of the window. Another face appears there,
nuzzles the little dolls ears. A little female face looks out on the

waste of brown water and doesn't see it. Looks up at the sky. Joe knows she is seeing figures in the clouds: donkeys, monkeys, elephants. The sun shines and the curtain obscures one ear. It tickles her, she laughs. Joe yells, "Look out!" The little girl doesn't see. The little dog isn't concerned. He bites the hand. The little girl withdraws her hand and tickles the ear of the dog.

Water slops into the window. The girl is so light she immediately disappears under the weight of it. Joe throws himself from the bank into the wild mass and tries to swim toward the house that shivers on its foundation. He gets to the window, floats into the room. Nowhere can he see the girl or the dog. He dives to the bottom of the room. He opens his eyes and shuts them and comes to the surface gasping. The mud makes it impossible to see. He floats near the ceiling, bumping into a crib, a soaked Raggedy-Ann doll. The water rises toward the ceiling. Soon there will be no air to breathe. He gets on the roof. The little girl sits there with her dog. All around trees are uprooted with their matted roots in the air looking like mops sweeping the sky. But the sky remains dirty, reflecting the water.

"This is the place where everything starts and comes to an end," Joe cries to the little girl.

"Do you want to play with my dog?" she asks. "My name is Teresa. What's yours?"

"Joe. It's Joe. Do you know me? I'm Joe."

"No, I don't know you, but you're nice."

"Don't you see what's going on all around? It's a flood and I've got to get you out of here!"

Teresa opens little round eyes of surprise. "It's a beautiful day, Joe. Come and play with my puppy. My mother and father will be back soon. They haven't gone far. They're collecting for me."

"Why haven't they collected me, then?" Joe yells.

"It's the wrong connection, Joe. You're not the right connection, Joe. They told me that before they left. Now I think you ought to go too."

"Where shall I go? I can't leave you in the middle of this."

"Just leave us alone, we're perfectly all right here. What business do you have?"

"You don't know who I am now, but you will. You'll drive a Packard around and around. But not if you don't get out of here."

"I live in Sioux City, Iowa. That's my home. That's where I live with my mother and my father. You go back where you belong."

"I belong? The water's going to carry us away if we don't move." He lunges at the girl and forces her onto his shoulders. He grabs for a branch of an enormous Eucalyptus tree and swings them onto it. "My puppy," she screams. "You've left my puppy."

"Too late," yells Joe over the roar. "I've got to save us."

"You've saved the wrong one," she cries, growing smaller in his arms, whining and clawing. Far away down the broiling stream, Joe sees a little girl waving her arms to him, terrified in the waste of waters. He looks down and sees a small wet puppy dead in his hands.

# PART II

# ONE

J oe flicked the ash from his cigar onto the rug and frowned when he saw that the puppy had already made a mess in the exact spot. "Teresa. You're not taking the puppy out often enough. Teresa!" Where was the little girl? He struggled out of the easy chair and looked out the window. She was down at the stream floating paper boats. Joe smiled through his frown and put his sandals on.

"Where are they going today?" he asked.

Teresa didn't look up. "Oh, far away."

"Do you want to be there too?"

Teresa deftly folded another piece of paper—the good bond paper, Joe noticed—and settled two sticks and a pipe cleaner in it.

"Is that a man or a boy or a woman?" he asked.

"It's a lion going to help the bear."

"Oh. What's he going to do when he gets there? Who's after the bear?"

"The bad men want to make the bear leave the forest and get into a cage. They want to make him do tricks in a circus."

"How do you know they're bad men who want to do that, Teresa, my love?"

"You took me to a circus and I saw the sad bears in a cage. And they had to lie down and roll over and do all the things they don't like to do."

"I thought you enjoyed the circus. Bears always roll around on the ground to scratch their backs."

"Well, the lion will scratch his back for him. He doesn't need a circus."

Joe squatted at the edge of the little stream. The paper boat got caught in an eddy too far out for the little girl to reach. He looked at her for permission and she nodded, so he pushed the boat off and it sailed free. Teresa waved until it disappeared over the rapids.

"Someday," he said, "we'll get into a big boat like that one and we'll sail over the ocean and meet the bear and the lion where they like to live. We'll knock on their door and say, 'I helped you get away from the bad circus men and now you're safe and comfortable in your own home. Can we come in?'"

"Yes, you can come in, but wipe your feet first, if you don't mind."

"No, I don't mind. Shall I take off my shoes too?"

"No, just your left shoe. I need the right shoe on to keep the rug down at the corners."

"Oh, all right. Is there anything to eat?"

"Well, there's honey and there's berries and some grapes."

"But we're just like the lion, we need other things to eat. Don't you have anything for us?"

"No, I don't. I'm sorry. But I'll play the flute for you to get your mind off food. You can't think about food all the time, can you?"

"No," Joe said, "I'll try not to."

"You'll get too fat," Teresa said, looking at Joe's middle.

"I'll suck my belly in and you won't be able to see my belly button, wait and see."

"Where's Mommy?"

Joe stood up and stretched. "She's already down the stream and across the ocean waiting for us. She's been there for a long time. Someday, when we have enough money we'll go and find her."

"Did she really leave from this spot, Daddy? Did she go even though she knew we'd have to stay here for a long time without her?"

"She couldn't help it, Darling. There was a big storm, right here in the valley. And I tried to convince her she shouldn't go. But she thought it was time, she thought we'd be able to go with her, but she made a mistake, and now we have to wait until it's the right time again, and then we'll sail to get her. Where's the puppy?

"Paul? He's down with the gas station man. He's teaching him how to make a house."

"Paul made a mess in the living room again, Teresa."

"Oh, he's sorry. He was watching me out of the window and he got excited."

"Don't you think it would be a good idea to go clean it up?"

"OK." The little girl looked fleetingly at Joe. "Then are we going to go?"

Joe's heart squeezed. "Teresa, I don't know, but promise you won't try to go without me. I don't want to put ideas in your head, but promise you won't try. You aren't big enough to go off by yourself. Whenever it's the right time we'll go off together, you and me and Paul, but now Daddy has to work for a living, to keep us in the valley, and your mother wouldn't want us to leave without being prepared."

"O Daddy, I'm prepared, I'm old enough now. You said when I was five I'd be old enough. I'm almost five."

"Yes, but I thought I'd have a boat and enough food to bring to the lion and the tiger when you were five, and now it turns out we still have to wait."

"Daddy, it'll have to be soon. I can hardly remember Mommy any more. I don't feel good about it. When Mommy comes to me in my dreams she's different shapes all the time."

"What was she like last time?"

"She was tall and very skinny. She had eyes like searchlights, and she didn't look very happy. And she kept trying to grab one of my hands to take me with her."

"Don't let her," Joe said urgently. "She's a nice lady, but she's impatient, just like you." He looked around for some reason to change the conversation. "Look, let's go together and get Paul, OK?"

"No, I want to make three more boats. I have to make one for every year since I've been alive."

Joe scooped her up in his arms. "Sweetheart!"

"Daddy, put me down. I'm not finished yet!"

"All right, I'll put you down. But give me a kiss first?

"No!"

"Then how about going to a matinee?"

"What's playing?" she asked, suspicious.

"I don't know, something about lions and tigers and bears, maybe."

"It's never the same as real animals."

"Then let's play a duet. Let's go in the house and get the recorders. I'll play bass. Paul will howl."

"Daddy, did you hear me singing to the boats?"

"No, I just noticed the mess on the rug and came out to see what you're doing."

"I was singing a song to Mommy wherever she is with the animals."

"What was the song?"

"I don't know. I can't remember. Do I really have to go to school after summer is over?"

"You don't have to if you don't want to. You can stay here and play. You can read your own books and never go to school as long as you remember not to follow the boats. You have to trust Daddy when I say I'll take you when the time is right. I never lied to you before. I gave you the puppy when I promised, didn't I?"

She looked up at him as though he were naughty and stretched her arms to be picked up. "Silly Daddy."

"I'm a very silly daddy. You're my silly little girl."

"We'll stay here for awhile. Mommy will come back here for us."

Joe swallowed. "Mommy is never coming back here, Sweetheart. Never. Never."

# TWO

"Doctor," Joe said, wanting to smash the bland man in the face with both his fists. "Doctor. Tell me something."

"What can I tell you? We have to wait. We can only wait."

Joe knew he was going away as soon as he said that. It meant Joe would have to wait.

"The fever will break. It can't keep going up."

"You mean it'll swamp her if it goes up much longer. Do you want to put her in the hospital? Does she need oxygen? She's gasping and choking. I can't stand it."

"There's no use putting her in an oxygen tent. She's full of antibiotics."

"But you don't know what it is? You really don't. You haven't any idea?"

"Frankly, no. The specialist doesn't either. She's more comfortable here. She was restless and unhappy in the hospital. She's terribly attached to you." The doctor put a hand on Joe's arm. "She has her dog here too. A hospital is just no substitute for being home. But try to get some sleep. Let the nurse sit up with her."

"The hell with the nurse! What does she care. It isn't her little girl."

"What can I say? Watch her then. I'll be back this evening."

He left, his useless black bag swinging, out to the golf course or to his mistress. Joe stood at the window and watched his expensive black car pull away, a Packard, one of the last big expensive Packards, the kind that eats a gallon for every mile. What did he care? Joe saw that the back seat piled high with boxes—samples, free medicines, none of them worth a thing for his little girl. All poisons, like strychnine. He suddenly wished he was in the front seat with the doctor, smoking his pipe or a big cigar, laughing and joking about the last round of golf, or about how funny patients were. How could doctors know what it meant not to be able to breathe, as though under water and not a fish.

My little girl, he anguished, you look like a mermaid, but you can't breathe water. Let the sun dry up your lungs. Take out the water you love when it's in the stream. Drain away from that little hard-breathing heart, that little overburdened heart. Breathe clean and clear. He remembered how she used to sleep, breathing sweetly out and in from both upturned nostrils, clutching happily her blankets, her bear and lion. His little girl.

He turned away from the window and looked down to the faint lighter place on the rug where Paul had made a mess. The ghost of a mess. When had it happened? Was there ever a day with sunshine and the reflection of clouds in the sky? And boats floating away to Africa where Teresa the Mother was waiting for Joe and her little girl? Now, she'll have her for herself, Joe thought wildly. She'll have her after all. "No! I'll never let her have her," he said out loud.

"Daddy?" Joe rushed to the bed, kneeled. "What, Sweetheart?"
"Where's Paul?"

"He's out running somewhere. Do you want me to get him?"

"No. Mommy's been here. Why didn't you tell me?"

"No, she hasn't, really. Forget Mommy for now. Just think hard that you're getting better and better. Sweet noble little girl. Remember you belong here and not over there. We'll sail in the boat to find everybody you want to play with."

"I like Paul," the little girl panted.

"I'll call him. Wait a minute."

"No, don't call Paul. Daddy. Daddy?"

"What?" Joe cried.

"I know how to make good boats. They always float. I'm going to get on one of them."

"No, Teresa. Stay off the boat. It's dangerous there without me. You'll fall overboard and hurt yourself."

"I don't care if I fall overboard. I'll swim and that will be nice. You can come too."

"I can? You've never let me before."

"You can come too. If you behave."

Joe held her hands. He reached below the covers and took her toes. They were cold. The cold touched him with ice at the base of the skull. It spread like veins into his head until he felt giddy and numbed with cold. He rubbed the toes and feet. He let go and fumbled for the phone. When he returned the little girl was humming a song. He caught a word or two. "Mommy song, water song, boat song."

That was all. No voice. He put his head to her chest. He heard nothing. He could not find a pulse.

He walked to the kitchen. He took out the sharpest kitchen knife and plunged it into his heart.

# THREE

——————

"You still like movies?" the candy counter girl said, the remains of the Hershey she had broken off for Joe still in her hand.

Joe stood because he couldn't fall over. He was planted in the lobby.

"So why don't you just step over to the waiting room? Look how much time you've wasted. I don't mind the time, myself. I'm paid to dispense. But you're not doing your job. How many times does it have to happen?"

She flipped up the gate, walked to Joe and touched his arm. She took his hand and rubbed his chest with her other hand. "Does it hurt? I'm sure it hurts. Come into the other room. It doesn't take long, once you're into it. I can't tell you everything, but I can say you're in for a marvelous surprise."

"Teresa," Joe said. "Where is she?"

"She's always nearby. You don't trust enough. You have to have some faith."

"My little girl?"

"Water over the dam. I'm not unsympathetic. I was human once too. But time is going by at a great rate. The rates are going up. The ante's so high now that I don't know how we'll overcome it. And think of the cost of film stock, at today's prices. If you think for a moment, you'll realize you're not being punished, even as much as you might. Notice I didn't say 'deserve.'"

"You dirty . . ." Joe mumbled. "What a filthy. . . ."

Candy sighed. "You know what will happen, Joe? You want more?" She let go of his arm and went back behind the counter.

# FOUR

T he knife came out with a creak, like an unoiled door. He noticed that the hole was larger. The knife was advertised as "survival." That meant that whatever it was stabbed into would have a gash wider and longer than you would ordinarily expect, because the knife was beveled and shaped so that it would rend and tear, like a dumdum bullet.

Most important, however, it did come out, and the blood came behind it, he noticed with satisfaction. But at the same time he heard a small sound at the door.

"Daddy?"

He was afraid to turn around. He was hearing things. This was the real way people died, not from puncture wounds in toes or mosquito bites on the ass, but with survival knives.

"Daddy, can I have a glass of water, I'm awfully thirsty. I've never been so thirsty in my whole life. Daddy, why don't you turn around? I'm awfully thirsty."

Joe grabbed a kitchen towel from the rack and turned. Teresa in her little nightdress was in the doorway. She wasn't in her bed.

"Teresa, why aren't you in bed? You know the doctor . . . you're very sick and. . . ."

"Daddy, *you* look sick. I feel much better. I slept a lot. I told Mommy to go away, Daddy. Now we can stay here until you're ready. I'm growing up to be a big girl. A bigger and bigger girl. All the time. Let me see what you've got, Daddy? Is it something for me?"

"It was something for you, a present," Joe muttered. He found another towel. The little girl walked up to the sink and looked at Joe's face. Then she looked down to his chest where the spreading blood dyed his shirt and the little trail disappeared into his pants front and ran down under his pants and trailed away under the sink.

"Daddy!" The little girl threw her arms around Joe's middle. His brain registered pain but it had no meaning.

"We'll have to clean it up, Daddy. You don't like a mess on the floor."

"Yes, Sweetheart. Call the doctor. The number's on the phone. Call the doctor. Tell him to come very fast. And if I can't hear you when you get back into the kitchen, don't go anywhere. Just wait in the living room by the phone until the doctor comes. Just tell him I couldn't wait. Tell him I was crazy. Tell him I was too worried."

"About what, Daddy?"

"Don't ask questions now. Make the phone call, can you do it? Good. Go do it. Leave me be."

To be left alone. That was the best thing. The heavy tide coming in the ears. The tide roaring to take him out, onto the waves, heavy salt waves licking at his ears and chest, sweet, heavy with salt, heavy, dull, roar, pulling the angry tissues apart and back, finishing off, letting to. The best. Visions. Little girl by the phone, the doctor's office answering, someone coming.

Joe's draining brain registered who? Who? The doctor? That was nobody. The gas station man? Nobody. There was Teresa. God, Teresa, the Packard—no, that's the doctor's Packard now. It doesn't belong to Teresa anymore, yet.

Words: anymore yet, anymore yet, anymore yet—tide. He couldn't leave the little girl. He was leaving her. He had so much to do, now that she was alive. There was so much to teach, show, take. There was so much. He had to hear that laugh a million times over. That laugh, throaty giggle, and the catch of the little mouth in pleasure. Boats, sticks, dogs to tickle, bears and lions. All that pleasure. Her little body lengthened and straight, the belly gone and the button tucked in properly, a mystery where all had been out in the open before. They both had sat and watched it go, like the moon over branches of a tree into a cave of the mountain. With soft drinks and marshmallows.

Where was Mother? I told you, Joe said, gone. She went away and we'll look for her when we get older. You're older now, and you can carry me. What if I get older and you're not strong any more, Daddy? I'll be strong. I won't be weak anymore, I promise. I'll be good. Just come back, Mommy. Where'd you go? I *need* you. We both need you. Why did you go away? What's the time? Late. Later. When we need the time it's not that anymore. Through aspirins. Aspirate. Muscles like glass fragments rubbing against each other. Doctor, what can you? Do?

# FIVE

"If it isn't there it has to be here," the doctor said to Teresa.

"What happens now?"

"We get him to sit up." The doctor pulled Joe out from under the kitchen table where he had propped himself up and then fallen when the center of gravity returned to his solar plexus. Candy swabbed the floor with her mop. Assistant Manager stood at the door saying this or that to neighbors who surrounded it curiously.

(The little girl shouldn't be seeing this. What can they be thinking of?)

"There. Now he's in the position he needs to be in. Rope? Got any rope? No? I'll use surgical string then. Can't be picky."

"You'll have to be fast, doctor," Candy said.

"Of course. I'll have to certify him. But he's not there yet."

(Not where yet? Where are those words? What is that smell? Does it come from the hole?)

"Isn't that funny? The puppy wants to play with Joe's feet!" Teresa shouted.

Paul stuck his puppy's rump in the air, bowed and growled at Joe's feet. He yipped and pawed his nose. And backed off, hurt. Teresa took him in her arms. "What's the matter, Baby?" She looked down at Joe's feet. They were out of the shoes, washed, white with collapsed, marbled blue veins. "He's got glass ingrained on the bottoms of his feet!"

"Weren't you with him on that first voyage?" Candy asked. "That first one down the broken street into the restaurant?"

"No," Teresa answered, looking suspiciously at Candy. "When was that? There wasn't time enough for that."

"Yes there was. I monitored it. I saw it. I thought you were allowing it as the first vision."

"No, it means he got away before we got into the theatre," the Assistant said, returning from the door. "Doctor, how much time do you need?" He looked impatiently at the watch. "Damn, still not working. Does the kitchen clock here work? Teresa?"

"Puppy time," she giggled.

"Stop it. Grow up. Grow up now. That's enough. That was plenty."

(How fast they grow. You no sooner look around but they've outgrown five changes of. And then it's the kindergarten and you. And there was never.)

"I'm sewing as fast as I can. Do it yourself if you can, with all your experience," the doctor said, looking up with sweat on his forehead. "All these lights in here. With all the experience you people have as a team, can't you get someone to develop cooler lights?"

"Cooler than where you come from, doctor?" Candy giggled. "If I can keep my candy frozen you can sew him up before he melts. If he melts he won't be any good to anybody, will he?"

(Still figure. Mind's coming back. I don't want to listen to. Let it rain where. Let it ride all. Let go. Great wheel spoke.)

"All of the openings are now closed except the top suture. Now it's all yours, gentlemen and ladies." The doctor bowed ironically, straightened his white coat. Suddenly, he looked anxious. "Isn't anybody here going to offer to pay me for my time?"

Nobody said anything.

"For my time and the distance?"

Teresa solemnly picked up Paul and put him in the doctor's outstretched hands. He felt the puppy like a blind man.

"Has it fur? And a tail?" His voice grew terrified. "And teeth?" He flung the puppy from him. Paul howled as he struck Joe on the knee.

(And the music. Where has music played like the music here? No, I won't try to get out this time. Let them take me where they will. I'm too old for playing. I'll listen. They're right, of course. They were all the time. About the music it.)

The doctor stumbled to the door. Assistant held it open, tipped his hat. "Take care of the car for now. Leave it in front of the theatre."

The doctor ran down the stairs and almost stumbled into the brook.

"The bridge, you idiot, take the bridge," Assistant yelled.

The doctor stumbled over the bridge and flung the door to the Packard open. Teresa came to the door soothing the puppy. "Just wait, you mean man. Paul will take care of you when he grows up."

The doctor was waiting for nothing. He put the Packard in gear and roared off, thick black clouds following, then rising slowly in the cool autumn air filled with red leaves that drifted down to cover the prints of the tires.

Teresa strolled out and watched the Packard disappear around the turn. "Be careful with that, Buddy. It could cost you a packet." She was a slender woman of twenty. She felt her breasts. She looked up at the fiery leaves. They were crying to drop from the branches and drift to the ground, to be mulch, to be pattern, rained on, snowed on, packed down to be earth. To sleep. Teresa felt her breasts. They strained upward to the trees, nude of leaves, receptive to the breasts of a virgin. Spread branches lean into hands and take up the milk of her breasts, suck them and kiss the face flowering between the breasts.

"Teresa?"

"What?"

"We need you to chant."

"Oh, all right."

# SIX

Who are you?

We chant.

What do you want with me?

We chant: Strive after Good; thou art in danger; before pain masters thee; and thy mind loses its keenness.

My mind is what it always was.

Anger is the obscuring passion.

I'm not mad. I'm not mad at anybody. Oh sure, a few unpaid debts.

The wisdom of equality. Forget ego. All-discriminating wisdom will follow.

Not wise. I never wanted to be wise. I just wanted to stay in the theatre and watch movies. What wisdom?

The air you breathe, foul. Envy. Jealousy. Now for volition. Will to dispense. Let go.

I can't let go. I have the grass and the branch of a dead tree in my hand. My fist is its own master. The dummy in the show window beckons. Forget me. Cut me loose. Get another hobby.

O nobly born, remember the Great Doctrine of Liberation by Hearing and by Seeing.

I'm not nobly born, I'm Joe. I can see you all. I remember who you are. Teresa? Which one are you? Gandharva?

We chant.

# SEVEN

A ll melting. All going back to the furnace. The refrigerators fail. The 1/10 of 1% benzoate of soda does not hold. In the freezer dead bodies seep out from behind brittle gaskets. Muscle and rubber both decay, but at different rates.

Lovemaking goes on behind the counter on the freezer lid while air inside the freezer turns black and blows glass over the reclining bodies.

The Hersheys begin to melt, black-brown. The nuts stand out like milestones.

Candy can't be discounted. The candy counter girl, barking and shouting, but nobody buys it fast enough. Before it all melts, shove it into mouths that themselves will melt soon enough, just not quite as soon as the ice and cream.

Is this some trick?

A mistake. The team will rectify it. A new thing happens. The melt is arrested, the flow reverses, a new parabola charted. A rebuilding of Stonehenge, a new Stonehenge. It has no name, there is no name for it in the world, as yet. The new name is announced at the end of the new era, when it melts and runs out of gaskets to hold it in. Then it is named. But not before.

# EIGHT

———

The Assistant Manager awaits notice from Hershey, Pennsylvania, that the twenty-five cent bar is to be reduced from 3/4 of an ounce to 3/5th. Then he will turn off the main switch in the main power panel, where he alone knows the location. He will signal to the candy counter girl that it is done, so that she can expect all the rest and not exhaust herself with fruitless running about and frantic calls to the power company.

It is all arranged with the power company, a vested interest. They are in collusion, as Joe suspected. Also the telephone. The quarter will melt. It is still in his pocket, but the pocket is sewed shut. The doctor is a better seamstress than predictor of life and death. He has had his function long since predicated for him, though he never knew. He will never know. He operates the Packard. The plant, with its fossil fuel, will melt, not run and explode. All explosions are now forbidden. There is only so much material to go around.

Then why Joe? He is the material that is last to go around. The rules are set out in a language to be invented after all the literature is already written in it. The stone with the written rules will resonate with intelligence. But we do not know if that is the hallmark of the new (but already gone by) age. We do not know that. We know that the power of preservation, of hardening, of stiffening, of adulteration, all must be stopped. And the Assistant Manager has done it, at the main switch, on orders, indirectly, from Hershey, Pennsylvania; and it has happened.

Joe does not know, at this time. He is trussed up.

# NINE

—■—

B e fond of what is doing the torturing. (Orphan whose eyes are eaten by the offspring of the usurer as well as by tiny exquisite spiders.)

Be fond of dying because it is good for you. Joe? Now where are you? Seated erect, trussed like a turkey set for the oven. The women have done their duty. You were shot down by doctor, knife, singing sword, harpies and mermaids—all forms fever brings forth.

Knives are fascinated with flesh. Punctures are to atmospheric envelopes what falling in love is to blindness.

And the male confraternities. Are the doctor and the Assistant servants or masters?

The more Joe thought, the more the fish line cut, the more it cut into his body.

Joe thought about the Packard. To be in the Packard! It had never seemed such a joy, but that was the nature of joys once past, only then recalled as joy. As a pleasure, with its varied stinks, pollutions. Also its invariable and fixed surprises in the back seat. Paradoxes were joy-producing, like gas. He remembered fitting the whole of the Packard over his nose like a mask and breathing that incredible stink, composed of matter and Teresa. How old was she when it all started? Around fifty? But she never said a word about her age or where she came from. There were mornings when she was as clean as though a sandpaper machine had gone all over her. There were mornings when she was wrapped in celluloid with torn sprocket holes and her pupils revolved crazily with News of the Day, circa 1921. Rin Tin Tin danced and skittered just under her lids, using the underbrush of her lower lashes as natural cover. The garbage in the back, much less the trunk, pulsed like natural compost. Joe remembered hearing, only now, the birth screams of little creatures, and the sound of quick smothering mouths of larger ones like kisses endlessly and almost silently compounded. If the uproar grew too great, Teresa brought out a large flyswatter and laid about indiscriminately. Joe remembered never noticing. Why did he not notice? Would it all be the same now if he *had* noticed? Nobody told him anything.

A present and past annoyance, not bleeding then and not bleeding now—and when the Great Bleeding occurred, it was in the dark and not even during the main feature, merely a trailer of coming attractions. Why open one's toes in the dark? That was a great event in a man's life, not something to take place in the middle of an anonymous night, followed by a blank sunless morning of 75 watt bulbs, hands grabbing his feet, bumping his head once, twice, forty-nine times back to the rear of the theatre.

Cheated like the little life forms of full weight and volume, his package of cereal rattling in the box despite a disclaimer on the package.

What kind of a life? What kind of a death? Aggrieved, and what good reason to feel aggravation. Joe's heart contracted. No, it wasn't really a contraction. It was arrested long before, it was only the settling of a muscle that finally gave way under the needling of fish line. The doctors always do their work well, especially under pressure.

Well, then, where did he meet Teresa? She picked him up, at the corner of Fifth and Main. How?

"Come on in, I've got another fifth back there you can have."

First trick. There was a fifth, an empty fifth. Joe had looked at her in exasperation.

"I'll give you enough to get into the air-conditioned show down the street. Pick the one, but keep it that way."

Joe didn't know to ask questions. She looked sufficiently seedy not to cause him embarrassment. Or ask him about his past.

Joe's past. Do we have to bring that up? The whole old film book of the past? It was all there. It was available for Joe to look at now. Do we look at it, Joe? No, we leave it blank. The real world was the back seat, not to mention the trunk, of the Packard. Once Teresa had opened the trunk to get out the spare. "Keep your eyes away, Joe. Just grab for the jack when I hand it out." They were on a freeway. The cars were crashing on, by, with. Madness didn't touch Joe when the fifths were full. The feeling of the full fifth on the soft palate. Hard now. Or gone? Can this be asked?

It had better have been asked. Now trussed. Then none. Teresa. What have you done to me? Why do you make available all this superb market of my own trash? I loved you because of the anonymity of the back seat. I sat in the front like a king behind the four hundred horses that carried us up into the sky and down below the world and then docilely deposited me, gently let me down, at the place of the summary of events. Where I went in, paid the silver, and the girl gave me a ticket to be sliced in half, then through the lobby into the left hand side of the theatre. That was simple enough. To have asked questions, after the past was closed like a fist, that was impolite. Teresa did not require it. Only the Packard never stopped. Now that was clear. Never once had it stopped, either to put him down or to fetch him up. It was always revolving, winter and summer, with and without Ethyl, always going, always the back seat different, always the front seat the same, and Joe never asking questions, merely taking orders.

That was the problem. Teresa was about fifty years old, if a police report needed to be made. And she encouraged him never to repeat anything, not in the sense of gossip, but not even of himself. That was why when the images came up now, it was as though they were happening for the first time—such pain. To have to live, not relive the past events, even the ones that might have occurred, but didn't, because thinking them might have eased the need for them to occur.

What about? I don't want to ask, thought Joe. I still don't want to ask. I don't have to ask. It's come this far. I'm a net full of meat and I'm ready for the cooker.

But, surely, I was fond of Teresa? You don't travel and make mistakes with someone for so long without growing fond of them? In fact, Teresa, the word Teresa, the feeling of the dust on Teresa, that was what his mind was full of. The infant Teresa, the little girl Teresa—what a foul trick to make him redo the take. They would probably juxtapose the shots, one after the other, maybe one on the other, very artfully, as a training film. They caught him off guard, that was all. But now could they simply and summarily lift and dump him in the waiting room with all the other—victims?

No, he couldn't feel like a victim. But as the wind howled through the open and empty rooms of the house by the stream, he began to scream.

Calmly, without anger or passion. The fish line set up a sympathetic howl. He howled and the timbers of the house howled. The puppy Paul was shivering where he had fallen at Joe's knee. Abandoned. In the Packard he would have found a place, but here he was abandoned. Where were all the personnel of this job? There was no water in the stream, sluiced out by the tremendous wind whipping around the lips of the stream, like an idiot's smeared lips, the mouth in a perpetual howl, the eyes saucers with nothing in them, the balls also scooped by the fiendish wind.

That was hygienic—with a vengeance! No sand. Not a spot of blood even on the floor where before were pools and pools of it. Not a flood of water this time but of air. There couldn't be so much air in the world; some of it had to have been imported from hell and heaven.

Joe rolled like a tumbleweed banging into walls and doors and finally with gusts and fits the wind passed him out of the house and over the bridge and onto the road, obscured by fallen branches and clumps of shredded greenery. No, yellow reddery. It was autumn. Teresa had raised her arms to it. With their soft hair to the armpits, caressed, Joe felt, by no other thing than the air. But the air was a person in itself. It did things like a person. It slapped the face. It whipped the body. It tripped a person up. It was a god. Everything bent and bowed to it. It sent up messages in the air. It scooped out huge tunnels in the earth. It was a glacier, it carved ice castles. A whole world was being made before Joe's eyes.

Be fond of this? Forgive this? Joe became smoothed like a rolling stone in water without wet. At every revolution he saw another piece. The shuttered darkness every time he had his face pressed to a piece of the earth beneath his eyes. So the movement was jerky after all, very primitive. Joe was interested. Nothing had been like this.

Suddenly he realized the miles-deep burden of the scream here. In terror he saw that, unfolded, it was endless, it would reach the ends of the universe: all those figures, heroes and villains, landscapes and city terraces. He could roll on the carpet of images forever and never come to an end. The wind was generated by the inequality of life inside and outside the theatre, and Joe for some reason had been elected to monitor it. And so it was for that reason Teresa picked him up at the corner of Fifth and Main? Only him? Or could there have been even a tiny reason for *him*? A tiny one? His past?

No, he wouldn't think about his past. That was to let go completely.

The villains were plucking at him, shining lights into his eyes as the world revolved—light, dark, light dark—as he rolled with it, growing rounder and rounder. Still, nylon held. Synthetics were incredible these days, not like when stockings were first made of them, when gangsters bound their enemies and dumped them in bays and the victims sometimes actually survived, the material was so shoddy. This was good stuff, and Joe admired it as he ought.

The lights were beautiful; loving them took some edge off the pain. Hands plucking at his organs he put out of his mind. How? They were least aggravating. The main thing to think about was Teresa. Teresa in the car, Teresa by the stream, Teresa in bed, Teresa with silver in her hand, Teresa at the other end of a telephone wire, Teresa touching the back of his head with her voice, nothing before or after Teresa.

But the aggravation continued. When the Packard stepped on his foot, not with all sixteen hundred feet but with only one, as a reminder. But of what? Where was it now?

At the end of the corridor, which corridor? The left hand one or the right hand one? Joe opened a tiny flap of his mind to Teresa in another position: in bed.

"In Bed With Teresa," he read on the marquee. Which one was that? Lola Montes, Jean Harlow. In Bed With Teresa. Sunday mornings she brought the huge bundle of newspaper and held up one little hand to be helped into the bed. Not that one. She reached out a finger and Joe kissed the blue veins crossing like a country intersection on her wrist. She was only asking for a cigarette, but she got the hot press of lips on her veins. She flicked the lips and took a cigarette. That one? Teresa of the many arms that never stopped revolving? That one? Which one?

One. The veins crisscrossed with wrinkles, skin hanging with gravity, a hand extended for the vial, trembling with the need of all the flesh attached to the one hand; heavy, too heavy to send out the messenger toward bedtable, cup, and white grains.

Joe. Always there. Was that the past? Was Teresa always there? That was the secret. No, no secret. Just the dark and the light. And the flickering of a shutter that hurt the eyes, with lights of blue, green, yellow, and red, sharp and shaded, as he rolled.

To be fond.

# TEN

There were children's voices singing or crying over their toys and bottles, the voice of the brook, the song of the breeze, the vapor trails of jets that lumped into musical notations. Voices of friends saying, yes, I'll have my sandwich with mustard, no, I don't want mayonnaise. The crunch and bite of a car's wheels turn in loose gravel. Birds telling the time of year by the way they sang.

Silence running through the tape like mercury, dripping time's plasma into the needle of the present. The sound not on tape of exploding synapse, of veins gone flat. Sweat that formed on lips spoke to the air that carried to the microphone: laughing.

Flies eating precisely where blood runs close to the surface, where skin is broken in some minor event. A little round capsule of lead traces a passage from a carbon dioxide vial under compression. Sound under compression like fossil fuel explodes, gasoline under pressure exploding in valves.

All the noises and the tape come to an end together in silence, snuffer on the candle. Instant off. Stopped, every one, all at once.

# ELEVEN

R ead me and live. Read only me. Be blind for once and feel the indentations. Leave surface alone. Leave surface for garbage collectors. Throw away the knife.

Joe, run your fingers over the indentations—confusing relics, but they can be read. Forget the other lights. Don't hold the paper up to the light. What light? It is a whirligig.

The living do come from the dead. It is only in the reading. Joe, if you desire it, so it will be. The chalice of skull brimming with blood is not the paper. Forget that. It does not exist. It is not your skull. The paper is not made of your skull. Forget it.

Do not dwell on Teresa, Mother-to-Be. She is not readable. She is sifting sand, the wind carries her like chaff, she gets into the sockets that you must allow to be engraved with truth. She plucked your eyes out. Now your skull is clean. It was always a chalice of blood, even when you were in it. Do not regard it now that you are at some distance from it. Come away. And your daughter, another trap. Let go of her small fat fingers. Your blood runs in them, playfully. Smile at the play of small fat fingers, but let go of them. Take away your thumb and forefinger. Make instead a sign in the air against the infernal wind.

The blood-drinking goddess does not have a tablet of the laws on her. She has lips. Do not regard what she does with them below your sight-line. Think instead on the goddess who carries the Law and whose lips speak signs. The other side of her will tell you truth. Read and live.

Disregard the image of your decay and falling away. Think instead of the parachute and its silk. Climb the lines of the parachute to the ballooning silk, now nylon and durable, and read in its surface the truth. Do not become entangled in the lines. Do not think of the earth rushing up to meet you. You have enough time to cover the soft silken skin in your descent. It is all in order. Learn to read. The hub is available somewhere on the surface. Think of the reading before you meet danger. Then will come escape.

Do not wander. Take hold of the lines and guide the descent. Find the proper draft. The line will go up, not down. You can find the up-draft. That is the truth.

They wait for you. We are not permitted to say who, or what the names are. A reception is planned. Will you be there? Read quickly, without panic.

You must learn to read the crackling noises, the use of the new body, as an infant learns to breathe. Joe, learn to breathe, burning aside a little from the enormous furnace of air that turns you into another balloon without direction. Do not wander.

Do not let the Assistant, the candy counter girl, Teresa, Paul, the waiter or the other strange woman to breathe into you. Breathe into yourself. Never let them guide you. Learn to read by yourself. Shut off the light.

The parachute flies in no-place. The airplane is gone. The vial is empty. There is no color. Do not look down. The glass swims in broken pieces down below. Do not look there. You do not want to be lost. Don't let the crystals of ice accrete on your sublime body, don't grieve for the memory of ribcage over cardiac.

They do not want you to think of them. That is why they change so often, take you so many different places, confuse you with rich foods. They do not want to be remembered. They have regularized you into a ball so that you might not come split in half. Now you float and you may learn to read. Read.

Your flesh has been eaten aloft by graceful birds, hammered to bits and deposited into small cavities in the rocks of the funeral hill, mixed with flour and formed into a dough, and the birds have eaten that too. Would you scrabble with indignity to recover it?

Joe, now come the symptoms of falling earth sinking into water, clammy coldness as though your body were immersed in water, emerging into feverish heat, water into fire, your body blown to atoms, fire sinking into air.

The divine wind has set you as a needle rolling on a thread; do not slow down, do not look down, do not deviate from the equilibrium that sets you going. Clearly, something good is happening. Learn to read it.

Forget the anger, the frustration of not understanding. The wind is enervating. It says kill! and slay! It threatens you. It is illusion. It is a test. There is nobody else with you or about you. Nobody has injured you or forced you to this place. The place of the letting of blood from your toes is nobody's fault. Drop anger.

Learn to read.

# TWELVE

Anger, but not Paul, Joe thought, dragging his feet through powdery dust. The little dog clung with his tiny milk teeth to Joe's sleeve and thumb, growling and sneezing at the same time. Joe's throat contracted in a lump. The puppy. What does it know? Is that growl to show me than I won't get away with anything or to clue me in that it knows I can do anything I want, so it's being brave? What's more likely to keep it alive in this powdered waste? What's going on in its little doggy head?

"Hey, Paul," Joe said out loud, holding up the almost boneless furry thing. "Say 'gas station.' No? Say,'burning myself to death.' No? Can't do it? Well, am I supposed to do it?"

Joe pretended to fling the puppy against a vibrating tree trunk. The puppy Paul clung tighter to the thumb and actually broke skin again. Joe smiled at the yellow material that formed in the tooth marks. It was nearing time. Wandering, how long? In this place with Paul as his only companion, he didn't even bother to look down at his feet anymore. They didn't hurt. The cords were gone. The other people hadn't appeared in some time. He didn't try to convince himself of his freedom; he knew it was a matter of time before they regrouped from the dispersal by that unbelievable wind he had learned after a while to control, to increase the fury of, to make to go up and down and sidewise. Joe's wind. They would be back. Here was proof: Paul. But not by any choice, Joe thought, isn't that right? Paul was not any defined breed, but Paul was going to be all right, someday.

Then it came to Joe that Paul was with him for some reason. he couldn't remember when Paul came. The last "event" was Paul's bump against Joe's kneecap. Then the Wind, then the time after. Why Paul? An overwhelming affection for the foolish young thing grew in his belly. He smiled and his eyes welled until everything became even more obscure. His muscles jellied and slid back and forth like oiled pistons. He could not support his weight, and so dropped to his knees holding the puppy in both hands, reverently, devotionally, toward the smeared sun. How beautiful it was to be allowed to love something with all one's heart, with one's soul. It was a gift. Joe praised the Lord with all his heart and devotion. His hands were heavy. The growling was less playful. Joe opened his eyes and the mastiff Paul turned his muscular neck at the same time. Joe narrowly missed losing his eyes and nose, flinging the dog away just in time. Paul immediately turned and attached himself to Joe's right instep, crushing all the bones. Paul then began pulling Joe's body toward the village from which came a babble of dogs' voices.

"Paul," Joe said, "this is not doing you a world of good. It isn't. I told you before. I understand the problem. I will have to stop it."

Joe reminded himself of Teresa and the Packard and Paul was left snapping his jaws in air, a look of terrified amazement on his face. He ran with his long tail between his legs back to the village and companions.

"No, I'm not a ghost. No, not yet. I won't be if I have anything to say about it. But I must find Teresa. That's all I want, that's the first and last thing. She will know how to make this episode end. I don't even know how far I am from the City. From the Theatre. From the Packard. This does require prayer. I wonder if it's a proper prayer, so I won't get bitten?"

The church appeared. Workmen were slapping it with concrete wrecking-balls, with winches and with bulldozers. The church took each blow with a flush. Priests were standing about with censers and had already founded small wailing walls of destroyed outer buttresses.

Joe smiled a greeting to the church. He walked over to the man running the show. "Here's my union card, Buddy, I'm qualified. Let me knock down one of those walls for a minute while you take a break."

The man said, "Sure, Mac, help yourself, but leave some for me." He pulled himself and his belly down from the catapult. Joe had never run one of these things before. He ran his fingers down one line of controls. The mechanism surged into tremendous activity. The ball began swinging at the end of its metal tether, around and around, like a stone in a sling. The man Joe had replaced yelled but couldn't get near the machine. Joe touched another rank of buttons and the concrete ball leveled out and smashed the bells and bell tower in one blow and then took out all the confessionals as it dropped, and in one final movement broke the altar. Joe stepped down.

"Hey, Mac, you got real technique. I didn't think you knew what you were doing, but I got to hand it to you," the man said, his face reflecting Joe's. "Sure, you're right." He smiled again and put his hand out, not as though he were going to shake hands but to touch the thing that was Joe. Joe moved forward so that the man could touch his chest. "Yeah, that's it," the man said. "Thanks, Mac. Come use my ball any time you want to. Say, you want a job?"

"I can't take on any more work right now," Joe answered. "But I won't forget."

"Yeah, Mac, don't forget. So long." He climbed back into his cabin. "So long."

That makes it not far from the theatre. Well, walking isn't so bad. Not if he could do what he wanted. That made two: the church and Paul. Paul, Joe reflected, was not reliable. Of all the helpers, he was the least reliable. Why? Because his job was least altruistic. He hadn't reached very high to be put there, and he failed when he got there. Terrible that little puppies become bloodthirsty mastiffs. And anonymous. Joe shivered. Anonymous. He couldn't get that out of his head.

# THIRTEEN

A girl about twelve came out of a house, pushed by her mother, who smiled and disappeared again when Joe came up to the fence.

"Hello, little girl," Joe smiled.

"Hello yourself, big fellow. " She was small, but her breasts were already formed and obvious under her gauzy see-through blouse. "Where you going?"

"To the city, to see my theatre," Joe answered.

"Don't you want to come in here and see what we've got?" she asked.

"What do you have?"

For answer she raised her dress and showed Joe her almost hairless pubis. She turned around and displayed her firm buttocks. "This is only part of it. My mother helps and you can do whatever you like."

Joe smiled. "That's very nice. Come here. Let me look closer."

"Sure." She moved closer, smiling, displaying the most beautiful even and dazzling white teeth Joe had ever seen.

He touched the length of her nylon-covered thigh, moving his finger in her pubis. He turned her in both hands and kissed the back of her neck.

"You're beautiful, my little lovely. Now, would you kiss with your teeth my left knee?"

"Of course," she said and bent.

"With your teeth," Joe repeated. "Don't forget the teeth." Then Joe prayed: "Let there bloom here the great tree of the universe."

The girl's teeth snapped at Joe's knee, and as he pulled away, snapped higher trying to separate the sex from his body.

"Peace be with you," Joe said, as he moved down the dusty powdery path. The girl backed into her garden, smiling with a green gangrenous mouth, mouthing words Joe could not hear but imagined.

Then he stopped. His mouth fell open. He looked back, dropping tears. "If that was Teresa, my own daughter?" He almost ran back to ask her name. Instead he stood stock still, trying to put that face and his daughter's face in one frame, but frames went by too rapidly. All girls' faces were the same. "How will I distinguish one from another, the right from the wrong?" He didn't know.

"My daughter, whoring at the side of the road?"

# FOURTEEN

"This is all too easy," Joe thought. "Something will get me."

He came onto a busy street. He saw the theatre. Through a glass he saw the ticket girl and Assistant Manager tearing tickets. He thought he could see the candy counter girl busy with her new bars of refrigerated candy.

Joe was so glad that he ran the blocks between, dodging the traffic of heavy trucks, ignoring the screams of drivers and policemen who had to slam on their brakes and who shrilled their whistles at him. He was going to be in the theatre again! After all this time. The ropes were off! How he would welcome even that bald-headed, oily and disgusting Assistant Manager!

With that thought, he looked again, and the theatre was gone. There were other theatres, but where the real theatre had stood was an empty hole in the frontage of the street, a sign advertising so-and-so, the agent for a long-term lease.

Joe pulled up short. "Be fond . . ." he remembered. "Be not angry . . ." he remembered. Of course he remembered. But that bastard! and the episode of the quarter and his sewn-shut clothes. Surely he had played foul, had not explained *why* he *wanted* to take the role. "You weren't God!" Joe yelled at the empty place.

A policeman came by and tapped Joe on the shoulder. "Easy, Mac. Don't blow up a storm."

Joe turned to him. He put a hand on the policeman's sleeve. "Please, Sir, when did it go?"

"That? Oh, that's been gone for years. Since the murder."

"What murder? There was a murder in that theatre? I used to go there every day."

"You haven't been around for a long time, that's easy to see. Sure, there was a gory murder in there. Some guy, an old hermit, used to go in there, and the bunch of them that ran the theatre hatched a scheme to get him, find out where he kept his money, and get rid of him. Sure."

The policeman was very pleased. Joe slowly removed his hand.

"How did they kill him?"

"It was a mess. They tortured him to find out where the money was, and then they let him bleed to death through the night until morning and then they reported it.

"A suicide."

"Right. They reported it a suicide. Damned clever."

"What happened?"

"Oh, one of them, one of the people in the conspiracy, he told."

"Who?"

"I don't remember the name. Someone didn't work there. A great case."

"Was it certain? I mean, did they really prove that the man didn't commit suicide?"

"You got some special interest in it? Sure, they went to court, they were convicted, they were all sentenced to die."

"And they died?"

"Sure they did. That's justice. And then they tore down the theatre for urban renewal. That's what's going on all around here."

"Thank you, officer," Joe said.

He walked the remaining steps, bent his head, looked at the curb. Teresa smiled at him from the Packard.

"I'll pick you up in the morning."

Joe smiled. "I love you."

"Don't forget. The Packard doesn't wait. You've got to be here on time."

"I'll be here, you don't have to make an issue of it."

"Good afternoon, Sir," the Assistant Manager said, his head shining with goodwill.

"Yes," said Joe. "I see that it is. I'll go in. And you'll do it, and we'll make it together, is that it?"

The Assistant smiled, not responding to Joe's words. "It's a good triple feature, Sir. I'm sure you'll find the triple feature satisfactory."

"Just tell me this, "Joe said. "Does she—" indicating the candy-counter girl—"have any interest or knowledge of it all?"

"Sir, she just does her job."

"And the projectionist, does he know how he piles it up on the screen? Does he know that someone has to come in and clean it all up on the screen? Does he know that someone has to come in and clean it all up by letting out the tiredness?"

"Everybody is in tip-top shape, Sir. Nobody is tired."

"I see," Joe said. "OK, I don't expect to know anything for sure."

"The left-hand entrance, Sir, if I may suggest it," the Assistant Manager said.

"To the theatre or to the lounge?"

"First to the theatre, and then to the lounge."

Joe began to walk.

"And Sir," the Assistant continued. "Just as a special gift, here is a whole Hershey, unopened, with nuts, as a gift for you."

"For me?" Joe flushed. He looked the Assistant Manager and the candy counter girl in their faces. He found deep smiles, bone deep, bedrock. "Thank you. Now I'll go in."

# NEW AMERICAN FICTION SERIES
Published by Sun & Moon Press

Winner of the Carey-Thomas Award for the
Best Example of Creative Publishing

1 WIER & POUCE, Steve Katz  ($16.95;$10.95)
2 MANGLED HANDS, Johnny Stanton  ($15.95;$10.95)
3 NEW JERUSALEM, Len Jenkin  ($10.95)
4 CITY OF GLASS, Paul Auster  ($13.95)
5 GHOSTS, Paul Auster  ($12.95)
6 THE LOCKED ROOM, Paul Auster  ($13.95)
7 BLOWN AWAY, Ronald Sukenick  ($16.95;$10.95)
8 THE MEMOIRS OF THE LATE MR. ASHLEY, Marianne Hauser
   ($11.95)
9 COUNTRY COUSINS, Michael Brownstein  ($11.95)
10 FLORRY OF WASHINGTON HEIGHTS, Steve Katz
   ($15.95;$10.95)
11 DREAD, Robert Steiner  ($15.95;$10.95)
12 FAMILY LIFE, Russell Banks  ($15.95)
13 PAINTED TURTLE: WOMAN WITH GUITAR,
   Clarence Major  ($14.95)
14 THE SEA-RABBIT, Wendy Walker  ($16.95;$11.95)
15 THE DEEP NORTH, Fanny Howe (paperback, Sun & Moon
   Classics: 15)  ($9.95)
16 HOTEL DEATH AND OTHER TALES, John Perreault
   ($16.95;$10.95)
17 MUSIC AT THE EVENING OF THE WORLD, Michael Brownstein
   ($15.95;$10.95)
18 METAPHYSICS IN THE MIDWEST, Curtis White  ($15.95;$10.95)
19 THE RED ADAM, Mark Mirsky  ($10.95)
20 A FREE MAN, Lewis Warsh  ($12.95)
21 THE PETRUS BOREL STORIES, Tom Ahern  ($10.95)
22 THE FORTUNETELLER, Mac Wellman  ($11.95)
23 TAR BEACH, Richard Elman  ($12.95)
24 THE HARRY AND SYLVIA STORIES, Welch Everman  ($12.95)
25 PRICE OF ADMISSION, Sam Eisenstein  ($12.95)
26 THE CRIMSON BEARS, PART I, Tom LaFarge  ($13.95)
27 THE IDEA OF HOME, Curtis White  ($12.95)
28 MY HORSE AND OTHER STORIES, Stacey Levine  ($11.95)